The Black

A Billionaire Fake Marriage Interracial Rom-Com

BY

T.L.Martin

Table of Contents

Author's Note

A story can come from anywhere. And for me, nothing was truer. Constantly seeking 'the story' behind every situation, I was instantly inspired by the viral TikTok trend, 'Black Wife Effect.' There were so many beautiful couples that made me say to myself, "There has to be a story there." And so I wrote one.

It may have seemed odd that I would write an interracial romance when my most recent release was unapologetically black...blackity black. But you'd have to learn a bit more about me to understand why this type of story came so naturally to me. Why it resonated with me.

I grew up in a blended home with a white step-father, my black mother, my two brothers and adopted cousin. My upbringing was a rich tapestry of cultures and experiences. I grew up listening to music ranging from Gospel groups like The Winans and Commissioned to R&B legends like Jodeci, and even Classic Rock bands like Pink Floyd and Chicago. I played the trumpet in the band, played the drums at church (your girl could play a full set), and acted on stages growing up as a child. This eclectic mix of experiences instilled in me a deep love for learning about people's lives that fueled my writing in ways I could never have imagined.

The Black Wife Effect was what I called my "palette cleanser" story as I ventured into true dark romance territory with my next series, Friends of Fury. So while this book is labeled as a dark billionaire romance, and Timantha and Will's story will feel very similar to a traditional dark romance, my primary goal in writing this was to provide you with a fun, summer read ahead of the danger and debauchery coming from the Fury series in the Fall of 2024.

Kidnapping aside, I hope this story will make you laugh and swoon at the magnetism of Mr. Will Huntley and the witty shenanigans of Timantha Spellman.

Visit TaccaraMartin.com for more information.

Chapter One

Timantha

There was nothing I looked forward to more than my book club meetings with my girls. When it started in 2017, my ex-husband used to say it was an excuse for me and all my girlfriends to get together and "day drink." *And he would have been correct.* But after 2020, when we were all forced to be alone with ourselves, and toxic men of all shapes and sizes learned how to purchase podcast mics, something amazing happened. We all *actually* started reading!

Since many of the ladies in my book club were also my sorority line sisters, we naturally started with self-help books designed to help us "level up." We read books about money management, investing, and becoming the best versions of ourselves while balancing work and family life. But when one of my line sisters pointed out that women had been fed these types of books simply to advance the agenda of the patriarchy, while allowing men to believe they had no work to do of their own, we decided to rebel. We ditched the self-help section and took a deep dive into the world of romance.

Initially, we started out with lighthearted stories from authors who wrote clean, wholesome romance. We would meet and talk about how we wished men would embrace chivalry and listen to R&B again so they could learn how to be better lovers. To spice things up a bit, I introduced the ladies to Kim Roby and her Reverend Curtis Black series, which they couldn't get enough of. Little by little, we all began to secretly fall in love with these unapologetic bad boys.

Seeing that the ladies were open to falling in love with toxic book boyfriends like Curtis Black, my best friend, Autika, introduced us to the smutty, intense side of contemporary romance—dark billionaire romance and dark mafia romance novels. The men in these stories were anything but chivalrous, and we all loved them too. Even though I often had to challenge some of the female characters' decision-making abilities, their enthusiasm for these dangerous and alluring male leads was contagious.

"I just don't get it. If these women really wanted to escape, they would have found a way! Are you telling me that just because a man is tall, muscular, and talks like the beast from Beauty and the Beast, you'd be okay with being his captive and falling in love with him?" I asked at this month's book club meeting, questioning yet another female lead's decision to stop resisting the advances of her mafia prince captor. Even though she'd just seen him blow a man's head off.

The ladies exchanged knowing glances, mischievous smirks spreading across their faces before they collectively chorused, "Hell yeah!" We all burst into laughter.

"Absolutely hopeless," I said, shaking my head.

Autika returned from the kitchen after refilling her glass of sangria and chimed in, "Tim, you always act like you're shocked at these women's choices when we read these books. Meanwhile, you finish each book before all of us whenever we start a new series!"

My friend Anastasia called out, "Let's not forget about the way Tim comes to book club with her books riddled with sticky notes and discussion topics!"

I smacked my lips. "Forget both of you! I actually enjoy our discussions, so I like to take notes for our meetings! And I finish the books so quickly because I'm always anxious to find out if I was right about the ending, so leave me alone!"

I had this game I played with myself where, whenever I was reading a book or watching a show or movie, I had to try to figure out what was coming next. Usually, I obnoxiously guessed out loud, spoiling major parts for everyone. But I couldn't help it. I had an obsession with predictability. I needed it, really. If writers couldn't craft a story where I couldn't predict the plot twist coming, I'd lose interest.

"I call bullshit!" Autika yelled. "I just think it's funny how you are the biggest critic of these romance novels but chose to start a business where you help people find love. Be for real, Tim. If not with us, at least be real with yourself!"

I hated when she was right. Of all my friends, and even my family, Tika was the one who could call me on my BS and make me eat my words. The truth was, I did love love. I loved romance and all the warm feelings that came with it, even if it meant embracing unrealistic expectations. But admitting it out loud was a different story. Saying it out loud meant wanting it, craving something so spectacular that it kept me up at night, consumed by thoughts of them. I wasn't ready to *let* myself want that.

"So, you're saying that you could never fall for a captor? A little Stockholm Syndrome sneaky link?" Autika asked, wiggling her eyebrows suggestively.

I laughed. "I'm saying these stories are unrealistic, but we love them because we all have a secret fantasy of taming the beast. But no, I don't think I could ever actually fall for someone who captured and claimed me."

Anastasia chimed in again, "I don't know, Tim! I think I might be okay with being taken away from a life of working and paying bills if some brooding biker took care of me!"

"Thank you, Stasi! I say all the time that there is a hard wig and a soft life with my name on it somewhere!" Autika screamed, making the room erupt with laughter again.

"You women are crazy!" I yelled, getting up to take my plate to the kitchen.

Romance novels were my escape from reality, but I was still a realist. I knew the stories weren't real, so I could detach myself from the idea that I would one day get my happily ever after. Yet, I was always intrigued by the kinds of women who could captivate a man's senses so completely, so deeply, that he would go to the ends of the earth to be with her. In the dark, smutty romance novels, the man would go scorched earth for her. And honestly, I found that to be quite sexy, even if it was totally unrealistic. There was something undeniably alluring about a man who would burn the world down just to keep his woman close.

Growing up with very little money, the library was my favorite place during the summer. I'd stay there all day, eating free lunch and burying my face in books. From romance novels to mysteries, I would get lost in stories that provided me with the thrills and excitement that money couldn't buy. Especially since we didn't have any. And even though I wouldn't dare share it with my girlfriends today—they'd never believe that the perfectly predictable Timantha Spellman was a daydreamer—I *craved* adventure.

Chapter Two

Timantha

This was either going to be a crazy idea I'd laugh about later or the best risk I could have ever taken in the direction of my dreams. It could go either way. I was starting a business at the worst possible time, I had just been laid off from my job as an executive headhunter, and Joe Biden seemed to be playing a sick joke by eliminating everyone's student loans except mine! The market was doing so terribly that my retirement funds, some of which I thought would serve as a nest egg, were much smaller than anticipated. *Naturally*, I decided to become a matchmaker for Atlanta's elite bachelors.

This wasn't supposed to be my life. I had a ten-year plan where I was supposed to work full time while being a matchmaker on the side until my business picked up. Once that happened and I had enough money saved to carry me for a year, I'd quit my job. Instead, the executive search firm I worked for folded due to the rising cost of hiring executives in the United States.

While some might have assumed I went into the field of matchmaking because I was a hopeless romantic who spent her free time devouring smutty romance novels, the leap from executive headhunter to elite matchmaker wasn't as far-fetched as it seemed. Similar to matchmaking, being an executive headhunter meant becoming intimately familiar with my clients' lives, their goals, and their dreams in order to help them find the perfect, long term career opportunities. It was sometimes one of the most soul-searching journeys you could go on with a person.

As a headhunter, I worked with both women and men indiscriminately. However, landing men in these executive roles tended to be easier, given that diversity at the top remained a myth. But working with men at this level gave me unique insights into their lives. I got to know the types of men who found themselves single and feeling alone at the top. They were powerful, successful, and yet, somehow, completely clueless when it came to their personal lives. It was fascinating, and more than a little bit ironic, that these titans of industry couldn't seem to navigate the simple act of finding a meaningful connection.

Against my best friend's judgment—hell, everyone's judgment, really—I decided to narrow down my matchmaking business to focus exclusively on affluent men whose schedules were too hectic to find a date, let alone a wife. Before I became a successful business owner (Leave me alone, I'm manifesting.), I encountered men who weren't interested in taking a wife for love or anything as inconsequential as romance. Most of them needed women to satisfy a contract or enhance their value in certain circles. Since women like me were rarely the subjects of such conquests, I decided to get a taste of this world from a different angle. *Besides, you couldn't pay me enough money to wear a hard wig.*

Desperate to find new clients, I printed chic, black business cards with my business name, slogan, and a QR code on the back. Then I left stacks all over men's restrooms and on tables at high-end gentlemen's clubs. I even had a friend of mine who worked in PR drop my cards in swag bags for an event that one of her clients was hosting. I made a mental note to remind myself to ask my new client where he'd gotten my information.

It was an early Saturday morning when I arrived at the upscale coffee shop, the Cinnamon Grove Grind. I made sure to arrive at least thirty minutes early to meet my first prospective client, Will Huntley. Forty-one years old, six foot two, and ... *oh my* ... a net worth of *$2.7 billion?* I glanced down at my hot pink pencil skirt and white blouse, suddenly feeling very underdressed. Why didn't I suggest meeting later in the day at a bar where I could have ordered a drink to calm my nerves? Now I had to rely on caffeine and charm to get through this.

I had thoroughly researched Will Huntley, and every article portrayed him as an elusive, philandering playboy. However, there wasn't much more information available about him. It seemed he valued his privacy. Rarely seen in public, Huntley was only photographed with women at various events, but he never gave interviews or speeches. It was unusual yet refreshing to see a man with such power and influence not broadcasting his accomplishments and wealth. Even if he was a player.

I had been using the camera on my phone as a mirror, checking my makeup, when a high-pitched voice startled me. "Another coffee, Ms.?" the young, preppy barista asked after I nearly shoved an entire stick of lipstick into my nostril.

"No, thank you," I said. I was jittery enough. I probably looked like I was on a blind date and actively being stood up.

As she walked away, my phone began vibrating. Smiling, I answered, "Yes, my love."

"Just your friendly reminder to give a big, fat F-U to anyone who says following your dreams is dumb. And if things happen to blow up in your face, you can always come live with me," Autika said. She was always there to remind me that life was short and to take risks.

"Thank you, Tika! You caught me just before my big meeting."

"I know! That's why I called! I meant to call earlier, but you know I don't wake up early on a Saturday for anybody."

I laughed. "Don't I know it?"

"So, who's the big client? Are you nervous? Do you think he'll like me?"

"I *am* a little nervous, and no, he is not your type," I said, shaking my head with laughter. Tika also loved the fact that I was starting an elite matchmaking business because she believed she was destined to marry a rich man.

"How do you know he's not my type? Who is he?"

"None of your business! Matchmaker-client privilege and what not."

Tika smacked her lips. "That is absolutely *not* a thing! But whatever. Hurry up and find me a man so I can quit my job! And don't be afraid to get a little something for yourself! The cobwebs are forming a palace around your vagina, and I'm growing concerned."

"Oh goodness, Tika!" I yelped, feigning shock.

I saw a tall man walking toward the door of the coffee shop, and I wanted to get off the phone in case it was Mr. Huntley. "Oh! Tika, I think he's here. Wish me luck. Bye!"

The bell above the door rang, and I was pleased to see the gorgeous man walk in. It was him, and his pictures did not do him justice. Very well dressed, meticulously tailored suit, and a watch that looked like it cost more than my car. I'd never dated a white man before, but this man had a Ben Affleck as Batman look going for him and I was digging it! *Keep it together, Tim!* This world was full of beautiful men, and if I was going to have longevity, I couldn't be fawning all over my clients. *But he wasn't a client yet!*

I stood to greet him, extending my hand. "Mr. Huntley! Timantha Spellman of Elite Harmony. Pleasure to meet you!" *That* was overly bubbly, and I suddenly wished I could do that all over again.

He shook my hand but didn't offer a smile or anything that implied this was going to be a pleasant experience. "Pleasure to meet you, Ms. Spellman," he said before grabbing the seat opposite of me.

The same bubbly barista came rushing over as soon as we sat down. "Mr. Huntley! So good to see you! Will you be having your usual?" I take that back. She was bubbly with me. With Will, she was downright smitten. Her pale skin was suddenly flush red, and a fresh coat of gloss had magically appeared on her lips.

"Yes, Maile. Black coffee, one sugar, and a pumpkin spiced danish," Will ordered with a smooth confidence. *Maile* turned on her heels and sauntered back behind the counter, clearly used to him and his usual order.

So this place was familiar to him, his domain. I couldn't help but wonder if he was the kind of man who required his subjects to worship and cater to his every whim. Would he expect the same from me? The thought made me both anxious and oddly intrigued. Because I could get into it. *Call me a sinner and baptize me in Batman's bathwater!*

All of my prospective clients had to fill out questionnaires and personality assessments before I even considered meeting them. It was crucial to ensure their goals and values aligned with my promise to my clients. Our slogan? "Where exceptional connections begin." I didn't want men showing up, expecting me to help them become some kind of suave player. Nor did I want them thinking they'd get a guaranteed "happily ever after" from my services. My job was to set the stage for exceptional beginnings—nothing more, nothing less.

Mr. Huntley's personality assessment revealed that, while he was seen as a strong and powerful man by those who knew him, internally he struggled with anxiety. It was why I let him pick the place for our meeting. If I had chosen a spot that made him anxious, he wouldn't have been able to open up to me. He'd be too busy battling the nerves raging inside him to focus on anything else.

Maile the bubbly barista came back and placed Mr. Huntley's coffee on the table with a smile that was way too enthusiastic for this early in the morning. As she pranced away, I had visions of tripping her just to see that pep falter as she smacked her little head on the floor.

"So I'm just going to come out and say it," Mr. Huntley declared, snapping me out of my murderous musings.

"I'm heading out of town next week to a business summit, and I need a date. A wife, really."

I blinked, my brain doing cartwheels trying to catch up. "I'm sorry ... a what?"

Chapter Three

Will

I woke up early this morning, my nerves jangling as I agonized over what to wear for my meeting with Timantha. Usually, my personal assistant would lay out a selection of the same suits I always wore. Today, though, felt different. *She* was different. I'd never used a matchmaker before; I typically preferred more *casual* arrangements. But there was something undeniable pulling me toward Timantha. Something about her made me believe she was exactly what I needed to make my crazy plan work.

My security guard must have thought I was a lunatic as I stood outside the coffee shop, watching her through the window. Words and thoughts fled as I observed the most beautiful woman I'd ever seen. The way she joked with the barista and nervously checked her hair was the most adorable thing. She was nervous, but it wasn't obvious. Outwardly, she exuded the confidence of a lioness, yet the way she incessantly bit her lip and adjusted her clothes revealed she was just as anxious to meet me as I was to meet her. Even if my reason was *different* than hers, it didn't change the very real truth I had been trying to avoid since the day I saw her picture on her website—With her, I was in trouble already.

As part owner of Veritas Consumer Ventures, I was responsible for attending conferences and summits to identify new business opportunities and technologies that our firm could leverage for profit. And since the economy and business world at large had been shifting, we needed new types of companies to invest in. I was attending a friend's wedding recently when I ran into Malika Conyers, the founder of Devine Luxe. Malika Conyers had built a small but successful hair care company that I was dying to partner with. They had cornered a market with virtually no competitors, and their projections were out of this world. However, Malika was known for being very particular about who she did business with. I'd heard she'd turned down several lucrative deals because the firms didn't embrace the community and values her brand was built around. If that were true, I had my work cut out for me. The only thing I embraced was money.

Malika Conyers looked absolutely stunning that evening, gliding through the crowd with her husband on one arm and a baby on the other. Watching her, it was clear they embodied everything she and her brand stood for—family, acceptance, and genuine connection. If I wanted to earn her trust, I had to show her I valued those things too. But the truth was, I hadn't been that kind of man in a long time. The cutthroat business world, and a private battle with a few public demons, had hardened me. I wasn't sure if I could convincingly play the part. Be *that* man. Still, I had to try something.

Malika wasn't going to be easy to win over. She was guarded, cautious—she didn't trust people in this world of business easily, and she was right not to. Small businesses were swallowed up and left for ruin every day in the name of capitalism, and I understood her conviction in wanting to protect what she'd built. Because she had built something that was truly remarkable.

When I saw her husband head to the powder rooms with their baby, I saw my chance to introduce myself. But my nerves were getting the best of me. I preferred email communication where I didn't have to think on the spot or come up with quick anecdotes for casual conversation. I liked to take my time, crafting my words carefully and saying as much as possible with as few words as necessary. Situations like this always made me hesitate before engaging. I couldn't afford to miss this opportunity, so I fought through my anxiety.

Clearing my throat, I walked over to her with the appearance of poise and confidence. "Malika Conyers. Will Huntley. Funny seeing you here!"

She flashed me a polite smile. "Quite the coincidence, Mr. Huntley. Especially after those enthusiastic emails you've been sending," she said with a playful wink. I'd been trying to get a meeting with her ahead of the summit, but her assistant kept brushing me off. They knew I was trying to get my foot in the door before other investors got the opportunity.

"How do you know the happy couple?" she continued.

I traditionally hated attending public functions, especially weddings, but Horace Norwood was running for public office, and he was someone I needed to keep close. "Horace and I attended grad school together. What about you? Friend of the bride or groom?" I asked, trying to find a common interest.

"I'm a childhood friend of the bride," she said, smiling, but offering nothing more.

She searched the crowd, and it appeared that she was looking for a way to escape me. Realizing it was inappropriate to discuss business at a wedding, and seemingly getting nowhere with Malika, I decided to keep things brief. "Well, I won't keep you. Just wanted to introduce myself in person. Will I see you at the Pitch Summit coming up?"

"I'm not sure. There's a lot going on. Our nanny is sick, and I don't like to travel without the little one just yet. Or my husband, for that matter," she said, glancing over to her husband, who was walking back toward us with their son.

Her attention seemed to be focused on her husband and virtually anywhere else but me. It was clear she was uninterested and unimpressed. I was used to it. As silly as it sounds, being an attractive man trying to do business with people more focused on kids' soccer games and family vacations than profit and loss statements always put me at a disadvantage. People in that phase of their lives usually didn't take me seriously; they figured I didn't have anything personal to lose if I was always chasing the next big deal, which wasn't *entirely* true. Still, many disengaged just like Malika was doing at that moment. I had to find a way to capture her attention and make myself memorable.

"Oh, I completely understand. When my wife and I start our family, I'm sure we'll be the same way."

Malika's expression changed instantly. She perked up. "You're married? I had no idea! Given the hours you work, especially from those late-night emails, I never would have guessed."

"Yep! Newlyweds! And sorry about those emails. I'm still trying to adjust to shutting work off at home. But my lady is getting me whipped into shape now that we're trying!" I lied, as I actively began cursing myself internally.

To my surprise, the lie worked. Malika's face brightened, and she opened right up to me, even taking a step closer. "Oh really? Will she be at the summit, then? People often look at us like we're crazy because we always travel together, but we just enjoy each other's company so much. As newlyweds, I'm sure you understand!"

"Totally," I said, shaking my head while trying to sound convincing. "The only reason she's not here tonight is because she's out of the country on business. But I'll make sure to introduce you two next week! Hey, we should grab dinner! And if your nanny can't make it, I'm sure she wouldn't mind sitting for you two one night," I suggested, quickly backing away before she could ask more questions like what my fake wife did for a living ... or *her name!*

"Definitely! We'd love that! I'll have my assistant email you my itinerary so we can link up!" she said. I nearly stumbled into the wedding cake as I was making my getaway. Now that I'd successfully made a colossal fool of myself, I had to find a wife.

A few nights after the wedding, I was entertaining young clients at a gentlemen's lounge a week ago when I'd caught a glimpse of a mysterious, black card strategically placed on our table. When I read the slogan, "Elite Harmony: Where Exceptional Connections Begin," curiosity got the best of me. The name on the card said Tim Spellman, and I couldn't help but chuckle, imagining some guy trying to summon the spirit of Will Smith from the movie *Hitch*. The intrigue alone was too much to resist, but I was also hopeful. *Could this be the solution to my problem?*

Immediately after scanning the QR code with my phone, I was both shocked and pleased by what popped up on my screen. Tim wasn't a man. Tim was short for Timantha. *Cute,* I thought to myself. Her website was professional, and her presentation was exactly what you'd expect from an elite matchmaking service. She had client photos, testimonials, and great brand photos of herself. *Really great photos.*

Timantha was exquisite. Brown skin, exotic-looking eyes, full lips—I had to reign in the thoughts I was having simply from looking at her photos. I needed her for her matchmaking services; anything else would only be a distraction. But one look at Timantha, and I wanted to abandon any plans of even pretending to want another woman, making me wish for something real with *her* instead.

My business partner and sister, Chloe, and I usually attended important business functions as a duo. I played the younger, relatable face of the firm, while Chloe brought her husband and played the happy family, giving us the appearance of perfect balance. Chloe was the one who was *supposed* to be closing Malika Conyers, not me. But when she went into preterm labor two weeks ago, I found myself without my professional wingman and the potential for this deal to blow up in my face.

I initially sought Timantha's help to find a date for the summit because my usual *companion* had fallen in love and suddenly had a problem with the charade. I could have attended the summit alone, but nothing seemed to scare off potential business partners more than the impression that I was a playboy or a bachelor. I needed to present myself as a responsible man with a lot to lose personally. And now, it would seem, I needed a wife.

Timantha was still slow blinking from my blunt confession, but she'd catch up soon enough.

"I will pay your twenty-five-thousand-dollar engagement fee that you require," I continued. "All of your travel expenses and meals, as well as provide you with a salary for the duration of the summit."

"I'm sorry, and what *is* the going rate for someone to be your *whore* for the weekend?"

"Week," I corrected. "The summit lasts at least six days."

She leaned in so close that I backed up in my seat. She stretched her eyeballs wider than I'd ever known a woman could do. "Do you hear yourself right now?"

"Is that a trick question?" I asked, and I suddenly remembered one of the last arguments I'd had with my ex-girlfriend where she said I was as emotionally engaging as a turtle.

Timantha began collecting her belongings, preparing to stand up when I reached out and gently grabbed her hand. "Tim, please. Hear me out," I pleaded, my voice tinged with desperation. "I'm sorry. I know I sound like a lunatic."

She scoffed, raising an eyebrow. "You think?"

"I promise, when I initially booked my appointment with you, my intention was to have you fix me up on a date," I explained.

She relaxed her shoulders a bit and took a sip of her coffee. "Okaaay. But?"

I let out a sigh. "There just isn't any time. The meetings I have next week … these summits are really important to my business, but some of the female executives tend to not take me seriously at these things when they judge me at face value. They either write me off as a slick businessman looking to get over on them, or they shamelessly flirt, looking for a hookup while they're away from their families. I usually have a date on my arm to counteract all of that so I can stick to business."

She smirked. "Are you seriously sitting here, with a straight face, complaining that women throw themselves at you?"

"No, that's not what I'm saying at all." I wiped a hand down my face. I was getting flustered, and I wasn't used to begging or asking for something more than once. "Timantha, I'm sure you can appreciate that appearances are everything. That … first impressions are the catalysts of any successful relationship. And next week, I need to make a *really good* impression. I don't need my appearance to communicate anything but a responsible man. Husband."

Her expression softened slightly as she listened, the initial tension easing away. I proceeded to tell her the pathetic story about why I needed not just a date for next week, but a wife. Surprisingly, she looked at me with kind eyes and understanding. And for a moment, I thought she would accept my proposal.

Then she flashed me a grin, took another sip of her coffee and asked, "How much is Autika paying you for this little gag?"

Chapter Four

Timantha

I should have known better. My first real client was a sexy, buff billionaire that wanted me to pretend to be his wife for the weekend? Yeah right! First of all, what man ... billionaire ... in his right mind hired a brand-new matchmaker in the first place? Second of all, what billionaire didn't have access to a plethora of women who would kill for the opportunity to be seen on his arm? I'd seen the pictures of the kind of women he dated, and there were no shortages of them. Third of all, stuff like this didn't happen to Black women! Like *ever.*

Mr. Huntley looked confused, but he wasn't fooling me. "Tim ... Timantha, I don't think you understand—"

"Oh, I understand plenty, sir. I just don't have the energy or the time to play these little games. Now, I suggest you collect your payment from Tika and tell her the little gag is up."

He let out a sigh. "There's no gag. I really need a date—a wife—for a big business pitch, Ms. Spellman."

I narrowed my gaze, deciding to change my angle for a moment. "So here's the thing. I actually think I may know of someone for you that would be available as soon as you needed her—"

His face lit up with excitement. "Seriously?"

"Absolutely!" I lied. I just wanted to see how far I could get him to take this little game because I knew it was nothing but

Tika and my book club girls being silly. *At least* they found a fine man though!

"If you would just indulge me in answering a few questions," I continued. "Then I could make sure that she was absolutely perfect for you."

He raised an eyebrow. "Okay? What sort of questions?"

"How long ago was your last relationship?"

"Five years."

"Okay," I said, pretending to make a note in my electronic tablet.

"Describe your ideal woman. Even in a fictional situation like this, what kind of woman *does it* for you?"

He sat back in his seat and took a sip of his coffee. He actually looked to be taking the question seriously. Then, he suddenly straightened his face and sat upright quickly as if he'd remembered something. "Attractive. Smart. Preferably educated and well-versed in various topics, especially global affairs. But she must have a personality as well. I need someone who can smile when I need a saint and sin when I need a shark," he said with a dark, sinister bend, and ... *damn. That was sexy.*

Clearing my throat, I said, "Okay. Do you have a preference for ... *race?*"

"No. Beauty is the only color I see."

"Noted!" I said, checking another imaginary box in my tablet. "And how old did you need her to be?"

He let out a huff. "No children or women near teenage years. I need someone in her thirties and preferably with a little meat on her. She needs to look normal, not like a supermodel socialite who drinks and snorts her meals," he barked, and that made me chuckle. "Look," he continued. "I need to know how likely it is that you can help me. Because if you can't, I need to consider other options."

So he was still in character, huh? "I'm sorry, Mr. Huntley. I just don't think I can. Your expectations and needs seem to be outside of the scope that I'm accustomed to. I hope you can understand," I said, trying to keep a straight face because this was going too far.

He furrowed his eyebrows. "I don't understand. You said a few minutes ago you had someone for me."

I sneezed, and Will instinctively reached into his coat pocket and handed me a handkerchief. "Thank you," I said, wiping my nose. "And I said that I *possibly had* someone. I don't make guarantees. But after a few moments of talking to you, I don't really think I like you. And I *definitely* don't have any women who would like you either." That was harsh, but I knew this wasn't real.

His voice became cold, his words measured. "Ms. Spellman, do you know who I am? What I do? Who I know?"

I tilted my head. "Do I—sir, I know damn well you better take the base out of your got-damn voice before you have coffee all over your little, pretty suit!" I said before sneezing again.

I stood up, fire and indignation in my stance. Then I hurriedly sat back down again. I was dizzy. But I shook my head

24

and stood back up. "Mr. Huntley, I'm going to save you the trouble and just exit stage left. I don't know what your deal is or what sort of game you're playing, but I'm not interested. In any of it. Please consider this my final answer ... go all the way to hell. Okay?" Then I stormed out of the coffee shop.

That man has lost his tall, dark, handsome, and fine-ass mind! Everything about that proposition screamed Pretty Woman turned Taken, and I wasn't falling for it. I didn't care if Tika was playing some crazy trick on me or if this man was the real deal. That was not the kind of *adventure* I was looking for in my life. That was a death wish!

I'd gotten to the end of the block when I heard a deep voice calling my name from behind me. "Tim! Wait!" It was endearing, hearing him call me by my nickname like that. He seemed so rigid sitting across from me like he'd never had a nickname for himself and only communicated in full sentences.

I turned around, half-expecting to see someone else. "Mr. Huntley, I am not sure what impression you got from me, but I can assure you that I'm not what you're looking for," I said, trying to keep my voice steady despite the flutter in my chest at the sight of him. Even with sweat beading at the crease of his top lip, he was *fine*. I bet his sweat tasted like the springs of life.

"You're exactly what I'm looking for. I didn't come to you hoping you'd find me the perfect girl, as if I was searching for a call girl or something. *You're* perfect," he said without flinching, his eyes intense and unwavering.

I sneezed again, suddenly wondering what had come over me because even though it was Spring, I never got seasonal allergies. "You don't know anything about me."

"Besides the fact that you're absolutely stunning, went to Cornell for business school, and you've mingled and rubbed elbows with some of today's top executives from your work as a headhunter?" he said, taking another step toward me. Either Tika did a really good character profile for me, or this man used his billions to run a background check on me.

Unable to withhold my curiosity much longer, I asked, "So how much *does* this pay?"

He moved me to the side as a couple with a dog passed by, then he held out his hand and gestured toward the park that sat across the street. "Walk with me?"

I hesitated, then relented when his hand touched the small of my back as he guided me along the crosswalk. His touch was nice. Gentle but firm at the same time. The raw sex appeal of his commanding stride was driving me to the edge of my resolve. If I was going to get wined, dined, and murdered, there were worse looking men to do it with!

We reached a park bench, and he took off his jacket and laid it down before allowing me to sit. "You're sort of unreal," I commented, laughing, before taking my seat next to him.

"Now, that's one I've never heard before," he quipped with a chuckle.

"You're just different than I would have expected."

He smirked while taking his seat. "I get that a lot. People don't usually see me outside of an office or boardroom, so that's the only side of me they're familiar with. And when the media paints me as some heartless tycoon or globe-trotting playboy, it's hard for people to reconcile what they think they know about me with what they usually learn after meeting me."

"I get that," I agreed, but I needed to get back to the subject at hand before I got lost in his steel-colored eyes. "So, you're willing to pay—" I began, my voice shaking.

"One hundred thousand dollars, plus all of your fees for your friendship for the week," he interrupted.

I gulped. Coughed. And maybe choked a little on my spit. "A hundred thousand dollars? For the week?" I leaned in closer to him, meeting his gaze. "Tell me what you mean by *friendship*?" I demanded, because that seemed laced with all kinds of innuendo.

"I'm not referring to sex, if that's what you're asking," he responded firmly. *Was I disappointed? No. Definitely not disappointed. Right?*

"By friendship," he continued, "I mean playing the part, attending the meetings I need you at, and helping me not look like an idiot at times."

I nodded, somewhat coming around to it. "I see. And where is this summit?"

"Do you have a passport?" he asked, a hopeful look in his eyes.

"Yes. But where is it?" I repeated.

"Paris."

I furrowed my eyebrows. "France, Texas, or California?"

"Well, since you'd only need a passport for one of those ..." he replied, a small smile playing on his lips.

An ambulance came wailing down the street, and it startled me so badly I jumped up. But when I got up, I got dizzy again, this time unable to reclaim my seat the way I had at the coffee shop.

"Timantha?" I heard Will say, but his voice sounded far away. "Tim, are you alri—"

Thump. I hit the ground, and then everything went black.

Chapter Five

Will

People's first time on a private jet was always fun to experience. They'd run up and down the aisle, check out all the cool compartments and ask what sorts of foods they could have while in flight. Since ours was an eight-hour flight, I ensured the kitchen was stocked with nothing but the best—steak, lobster, sushi, you name it. I'd ensure Timantha was well taken care of. That is, once she woke up.

While we were at the park, Timantha had passed out, and I was suddenly in the middle of a very uncomfortable situation. There had been an accident down the street, so police and sirens were everywhere. Once people noticed Timantha on the ground, a crowd began forming, and I didn't need that sort of attention on us—me or her. Thinking quickly, I called my driver to grab us and had him take us to my private physician.

After a thorough examination, the doctor determined that Timantha had an allergic reaction to something in the pumpkin danish I had eaten. When I touched her at the coffee shop, then again on the street, some of the ingredients transferred to her, triggering a reaction. I was faced with two dilemmas: ensuring Timantha's recovery and figuring out how I was going to get her to agree to come to Paris with me. And there was only time for one of those.

I had to think everything through. Once Timantha woke up, she'd probably assume I had drugged her, panic, and call the police, which would derail my entire plan and probably land me in jail. But if I could get her to a secluded place and explain everything one more time, maybe I could convince her to go along with this charade. So, yes, I kind of, sort of, kidnapped her. But in my mind, it was the more sensible option.

"Are you insane?! You're going to end up in prison with Dad! I'll have to run the company by myself, and we'll be bankrupt because we'll be paying your legal fees!" my sister Chloe had exclaimed. I had called her to explain my plan on the way to the airport and she had called me back in flight. Normally, I'd say she was overreacting, but as my right hand and COO, her concerns were valid.

"Chloe, just trust me. Timantha is a smart woman who will listen to reason. I'm sure of it."

"Says the man who has just entered international airspace with an unconscious woman he doesn't even know! Do you know what the maximum penalty is for what you're doing?"

I raised a brow. "No. Do you?"

Chloe began to whisper as if she was afraid of being found out. "No! And I'm afraid to Google it because Google searches are always the first thing authorities look at, and I don't want to be named as your accomplice!"

"Chlo, why are you whispering?"

"I don't know! What if your phone is bugged?!"

I laughed. "Well, let's hang up now before they're able to trace the phone lines too," I said sarcastically. She didn't find that funny either.

"I don't know how you can be so unserious about all of this when everything we've worked for hangs in the balance. When Jessica Lucas is *waiting* to strike now that she's joined a new firm."

Jessica Lucas used to work for my firm but left to join a competitor. But that's not the full story. She relentlessly came onto me, flirting non-stop until I had no choice but to report her to HR. I didn't fraternize with employees, nor was I foolish enough to risk a sexual harassment suit in my position. Consensual or not, relationships like that ruined great men every day, and I refused to be named among men who couldn't keep it in their pants.

Needless to say, Jessica didn't take my rejection well. She exited the company furiously, and since then, she'd been plotting her revenge for the humiliation she felt.

Chloe was my sister, my best friend, and my fraternal twin. We hadn't spent much time apart since birth, and we wouldn't have it any other way. When we were in college, our father was sent to prison for corporate espionage and embezzlement, forcing us to leave school and fend for ourselves. But Chloe had crafted a plan for us to work two jobs each, share a one-bedroom apartment, and put ourselves through college. Her strength and resilience are why I believed so strongly in investing in women-owned businesses.

I was reading through some reports when I heard a loud shriek coming from the back of the plane, where the bedroom area was.

"Sir, I believe she's awake," the flight attendant said, panic evident on her face. "Are you sure this is—"

31

I placed a gentle hand on her shoulder. "It's fine, Lydia. I'll handle it." She smiled, but my words did nothing to calm her.

I stood and began walking to the back of the plane just as the bedroom door swung open. Timantha stood there, her hair disheveled, eyes bloodshot, and breathing heavily.

"Timantha. I know this is not what you expected, but let me explain," I said, trying to keep my voice steady and reassuring.

"Explain?! Where am I? How did I get here?" Timantha screamed, her eyes darting around as she rapidly cataloged her memories from the day before.

She looked out the plane window and around the luxurious space we were in. I saw the exact moment everything clicked for her. "You drugged me?" she asked before launching into a full-blown screaming fit. "Heeeelp! Somebody! Please! Help me!"

"You're fifty thousand feet in the air," I said with a straight face, trying to keep my voice level. "No one can hear you."

"I knew I felt funny at the park! You bastard, you drugged me!"

"You had an allergic reaction, Tim. Calm down."

As soon as the words left my mouth, I knew I had made a colossal mistake. "Calm down?" she said, surprisingly composed despite the fire in her eyes. She looked calm, but her eyes looked like she was about to go full-blown Carrie on me. It was a remarkable contrast.

She moved her face within inches of mine and lowered her voice even more. "Did you just tell me to calm down?"

As a six-foot-two man with more money than Elon Musk, it brought me no pleasure to admit that I was scared. Her neck started rolling, fingers pointing and flailing all over the place, while she simultaneously gyrated her hips back and forth. I was mesmerized—and terrified. *Mostly terrified.*

"Be fucking for real, Will!" was the last thing I caught that she'd said.

"Okay, okay, maybe 'calm down' was the wrong choice of words," I stammered, trying to backpedal. "Let's just talk about this, alright?"

"Talk?!" she exclaimed, her voice dripping with sarcasm.

"Look, I panicked," I admitted, holding up my hands in surrender. "I just needed you to hear me out without you running off."

She raised one eyebrow. "And whisking someone away without their consent and putting them on an airplane thousands of feet in the air was the *only* solution?"

"Well, when you put it like that, it sounds bad," I muttered.

Timantha took a deep breath, trying to regain some composure. "You have exactly five minutes to explain yourself before I punch you in the throat and start throwing things," she promised, but her voice was shaky.

A tear fell down her cheek, and I immediately felt like the biggest asshole alive. "Are you gonna sex traffic me?" she asked innocently, and I couldn't help but smile at the rasp in her voice.

I held my hands up in a defensive posture and took another step toward her. "I am *not* going to sex traffic you, murder you, or hurt you in any way, shape, or form. I promise," I assured her.

I stepped to the side and pointed toward the area of the plane where the chairs sat. "Come sit with me please?"

She folded her arms and leveled me with a stare. "Last time I sat down with you, I ended up knocked out and put onto a plane against my will!"

I smiled. "There isn't much else I can do to you up here, Tim."

She eventually relented and joined me in one of the seats where we could talk. She sat across from me, her eyes sharp and wary. "Go ahead then. Talk."

"Safety first!" I said with a grin, gesturing to her seatbelt. "Buckle up. It's the law." I winked.

"Don't even get me started on the law," she snapped.

"Touché."

She buckled her seatbelt, and I took a moment to appreciate her form. Her presence was captivating, but she quickly interrupted my admiration.

"What the hell are you staring at?" she demanded, her eyes narrowing. Then another realization hit her, and she launched into a barrage of questions ... again.

"How did you get me dressed? Did you see me naked? Where are my things? What the hell is going on?!"

"Whoa, one question at a time," I said with a low, calming voice. "You're wearing a simple jogging suit my assistant helped you into. And your things are right over there." I pointed to the overhead compartment. "As for what's going on, let me explain."

"Three minutes!" she warned, her eyes still blazing.

"You had an allergic reaction at the park, and I panicked. I brought you to my private physician, who took care of you. Once he gave you a clean bill of health, I just wanted to get you somewhere safe to explain everything."

"So you thought kidnapping me was the best option?" she said, incredulous.

"In hindsight, not my finest moment," I admitted, scratching the back of my head. "But I needed to make sure you'd hear me out without running off."

"What did I have an allergic reaction to?" she asked.

"Something in the pumpkin danish I ate and it caused your lungs to close up on you."

"Nutmeg," she confirmed.

"Yes, when my private physician checked you out, he said it was likely the nutmeg, but he wasn't sure. He gave you some medicine to counteract the reaction and assured me you'd be fine."

Her face was still etched with confusion. "Okay?"

I chuckled nervously. "Look, you're a really organized person. So organized, in fact, that it wasn't hard for my staff to find your luggage, have my assistant pack your belongings, or get my security team to crack your safe where your passport was stored in your apartment," I explained.

She blinked erratically, clearly struggling to keep up with everything I was saying. "Rich people are so weird," she muttered under her breath.

"If it makes you feel any better, I didn't see you in any compromising positions. My assistant handled everything discreetly and professionally," I added, trying to reassure her.

She fiddled with the strings on her jogging suit jacket, her fingers trembling slightly. "That ... that actually does make me feel a *little* better. Thank you," she said, her voice softening just a bit.

"Then I drugged you."

Her eyes widened. "What?!"

"You were sleeping so peacefully, and the doctor said you'd be out for at least twelve hours from the allergy meds. I didn't have that kind of time, Timantha. I have a meeting in France first thing in the morning, and I didn't want to fly out if there was a chance you could go with me and help me close this deal."

"You're forgetting the fact that I don't know you, Will! What did you think, that I was going to forget about this stunt and suddenly be okay with smiling and pretending to be your wife for the week while under duress?"

"I was *hoping* I could convince you to come around to seeing things my way. This could be beneficial for both of us."

That seemed to get her attention. "How so?"

"I've gone through your website, evaluated your business model, and I think you have something that could work well in an app."

"I ... I know that! That's a future milestone I hope to reach once I build up enough clientele and word of mouth."

"What if you didn't have to wait?"

Her facial expression turned curious. "What do you mean?"

"What if you had an investor that was willing to give you the money to build your app?"

"I'd ask what's the catch?"

"The catch is, be my wife for the week, don't report me to the authorities when we get back stateside, and I will give you sixty-five thousand dollars to build your app."

She gulped. "On top of the hundred and twenty-five thousand you've already promised?"

"Yes. On top of that. And just to let you know I'm serious, I'm going to have Lydia bring you your phone so you can see that I've already wired an initial payment of twenty-five thousand dollars to your bank account as instructed on your engagement agreement," I said, offering my hand to her to shake. "What do you say? Deal?"

She looked me up and down, and I could tell she was seriously considering my proposal. I had to hand it to my sister. While Timantha was in the back sleeping, Chloe had sent me an email suggesting I add this little addendum to my offer. Chloe figured that if Tim was smart, she'd only agree to this arrangement if it offered her benefits beyond money. She guessed right. Timantha wanted an opportunity to build her business her way.

Timantha slowly, tentatively offered her hand to mine. "Okay, then. Deal."

Chapter Six

Timantha

He drugged me. This beautiful, Ben Afflecky man drugged me and put me on a private plane to Paris! Saying it out loud, it actually sounded sexy as hell. I had been transported into a dark billionaire romance novel, and I had the nerve to be upset about it! My book club girlies were not going to believe this! Here I was, living out a fantasy that would make any romance reader swoon, and I was caught between feeling furious and ridiculously excited.

Despite my excitement, I still couldn't wrap my mind around *why* Will needed this. Why he chose *me?* When I thought it was a silly joke that Tika and the girls were playing on me, the notion only made sense because it was something that we read all the time in our romance novels. But now that this was *actually* happening, I was confused. Did rich men really run around kidnapping unsuspecting women for real?

We were sitting in the area of the plane where a TV and dining area sat when I looked over at Will. He was reading the newspaper like my granddaddy, and it made me chuckle. "Just level with me," I said, hoping the exasperation in my voice would prompt him to divulge more. "What is this really about? Because I'm trying to make sense of it, and it's not computing." I cut into the steak the in-flight chef had prepared for me, waiting for his response, and moaned at the taste of the buttery meat touching my tongue.

"I have social anxiety," he said. My chews slowed, and I dropped the fork onto my plate. My heart instantly melted at that admission. "When my sister Chloe is with me, I'm fine. She's my business partner, but she's also a lifeline of sorts. The summit this week is a really big deal that Chloe won't be able to attend, and I don't think I can do this pitch alone," he confessed, his vulnerability catching me off guard.

I sat there with a straight face as he told me about his childhood and how he first discovered that he was severely introverted and suffered from social anxiety. "I was popular. I played sports. I had girlfriends. So my parents always assumed I was developing naturally. And I felt the pressure to make them believe that was the case. But I dreaded going to my football games and being around big crowds. I got irritable and depressed when I couldn't get time to myself. I had the hardest time making and keeping friends because I didn't have the language for the extreme anxiety I'd feel when it came time to hang out."

I had never met anyone with social anxiety before. I'd always assumed it was the same condition that kept people afraid to leave their houses. But sitting there, talking to Will, I realized it was different. It was hard to reconcile this strong, commanding presence with someone who got anxious around people. Yet, there he was, opening up about his struggles. It was kind of sweet, actually.

That was the moment I decided to give in and go along with his charade. I was still on the fence a bit, but this confession made everything real and gave me a sense of understanding. And I wanted to help him. He made me want to be there for him.

The flight attendant came to collect my plate, and I nearly fought her for the scraps. I had never tasted a steak that melted on my tongue like that, and I might have had a full belly, but I wanted more. I could definitely get used to this lifestyle. Growing up poor, you were almost afraid to want things like this, but after experiencing it, you couldn't tell me I wasn't built for it. Will just looked at me and smiled as I cleaned my hands with the little, wet napkins, a knowing glint in his eyes.

"What?" I asked, looking up at him as he smirked.

"Nothing. It's just that you'd think you never had a steak before the way you nearly took Lydia's head off over that plate," he commented, making us both burst into laughter.

Despite the current situation, I felt strangely comfortable with this man. Like I could share all of my secrets with him and he'd keep them safe for me. His large frame and intimidating gait might have scared most, but somehow I felt like I'd just seen a side of him that he reserved for only a select few. His eyes held a vulnerability that I couldn't ignore. He genuinely needed someone, and for some inexplicable reason, he had chosen me.

As the plane flew through the clouds, I couldn't help but feel a connection to Will. I didn't feel sorry for him or pity him. I empathized with him. Understood him, even. Kidnapping was taking things *beyond* far, but what was I going to do about it at this point, parachute out of the plane? This adventure, this crazy plan, might just be the change I needed. And maybe, just maybe, it would lead to something more than either of us expected.

"Alright," I said, taking a deep breath. "Let's do this. Tell me everything I need to know about being Mrs. Huntley."

Chapter Seven

Will

"Why do we have to pretend to be married? Why not *just* engaged?" Timantha asked.

"Because I'm an idiot who blurted out that I was married without thinking."

Timantha laughed. "And you did that, why, exactly?"

"The woman I was trying to impress seemed to only be interested in doing business with people who were more family oriented. I figured saying I was married would make me seem more like the kind of man she'd want to do business with."

"A liar?" she quipped.

"A kind, responsible man whose priorities weren't solely wrapped up in business."

She raised an eyebrow. "And that's not true? You're not a kind and responsible man?"

I let out a breath. "I'm a layered man. Kind when needed. Responsible to a fault—"

"Except when you're kidnapping people," she said, cutting me off.

I grinned. "Except for that."

"An engaged man is just as disarming as a married man. Even more so, if you were to ask me," Timantha continued.

I raised an eyebrow. "Oh yeah? How so?"

"A married man usually has all the complaints and stories of the old ball and chain. Whereas a newly engaged man is full of excitement and wonder. He can't wait to tell people he's in love!"

I furrowed my brow. "What kind of men have you been hanging out with?"

She smacked her lips. "I'm serious! Newly engaged men are some of the most jovial human beings I have ever met because they don't care to try to hide their joy!"

I took a moment to consider what she was saying. "The thing is, I don't *do* jovial. I'm much better as a brooding husband than a doting fiancé."

"Besides," Tim continued, barreling right through what I'd just said. "You're Will Huntley. A billionaire. Nobody is going to believe that you snuck off and got married without some obnoxious announcement!"

"I'm a guarded man. I don't give interviews, and I am meticulously closed off to the press. It wouldn't be *that* hard to believe."

"And what if someone decided to do a quick background check and discover you weren't married?"

My eyes flashed to hers. "You think someone would do that?"

She rolled her eyes. "Please, people are petty and vindictive when money is on the line. You don't want to give them any ammunition with something that is able to easily be disproven. An engagement works better for the lie."

"Fine. When we land, we'll get married for real. But I'm not doting. I don't dote."

"That was a *huge* leap! That wasn't a suggestion to up the ante of this deal, Will! I can't marry you!"

"Why not? We could get it annulled as soon as we're back in the states."

Tim folded her arms across her chest again, and this time I noticed her cleavage peak over her white tank top. "First of all, we are *not* getting married. Second of all, I don't *do* grumpy men, so you're going to have to figure something out about that." Noticing how what she'd just said might have sounded, she added, "Not that I'd *do you* as the doting fiancé either."

"Okay. No real marriage. We'll be married in title only. But I won't be calling you muffin and babe for this."

She narrowed her eyes. "You'll do whatever is required to elevate my performance, Mr. Huntley. I'm just going to need you to give me *something* to work with because I will not be seen even pretending to be married to a lame dude."

I stood there staring at her, willing her to meet me halfway. She responded to me as if I was being difficult, but that wasn't the case at all. I *couldn't* perform a certain way if my anxiety was raging inside of me.

Then her eyes suddenly softened as soon as understanding eclipsed her face. "Fine. I'll handle the couple stuff, and you handle the business stuff. Just keep your hands and eyes on me at all times, and whenever someone asks you a question about us, look at me and say, 'You tell it so much better, babe,' and I'll know to pick it up from there."

I smiled. "Like a teammate."

"Exactly like that," she agreed, smiling.

Keeping my hands and eyes off her was going to be difficult, but not impossible. Even if she was beautiful with a curvaceous body that was downright mouth-watering. I had excellent self-control, and I would exercise it furiously as long as she was in my presence.

Other things, however, would certainly be hard. The more time I spent close to her, the weaker my resolve became. This was supposed to be a business transaction, and I needed to remember that. But it was frustratingly difficult to keep that in mind when there was a king-sized bed just a few feet away in the back of the plane.

Her presence was overpowering. Every glance, every subtle movement she made, seemed designed to test my willpower. It took everything in me to focus on the task at hand and not let my mind wander to places it shouldn't. This charade we were playing required all my concentration, but she made it almost impossible to think straight.

"Maybe we should go over our backstory," she suggested, her voice a lifeline to my straying thoughts. "How did we meet?"

"So you'll marry me?"

"No," she said, giggling. "I said I'd *help* you! *Not* marry you. You must not hear the word 'no' very often, huh?"

I knew she wouldn't agree to it, but I enjoyed making her laugh. It was the oddest sensation.

"Very rarely," I shot back. Leaning in closer to her, I asked, "What do I have to do to get you to give in to me, Timmy?" My voice was a low, seductive whisper. I enjoyed making her blush too.

I saw chills cover her chest, and my eyes grew dark. I saw how she watched me. How she smiled in my direction when I wasn't looking. I wasn't proud of it, but I knew how to use my seductive powers for both good and evil. I wasn't sure which side this little game fell on, but it felt good.

She let out a breath and bit her bottom lip. "Ummmm … you can start by not calling me Timmy. My daddy used to call me that, and when you say it all sexy and shit, it ruins it for me."

I winced. "Duly noted."

"Let's get back to our backstory, shall we? Again, how did we meet?"

"It's always better to stay as close to the truth as possible. You're a professional matchmaker and I sought you out for your assistance. However, one look at you, and I knew I didn't want anyone else," I said, watching her cheeks flush despite her rich brown complexion.

Timantha cleared her throat, her hand aimlessly caressing her neck and then her collarbone. She wasn't just blushing; she was flustered. The sight of her touching herself sent a jolt through me.

"And that's the truth?" she asked, her voice soft and breathy.

I wet my bottom lip, my gaze locked on hers. "Close."

"And," she continued, her nerves making her voice barely above a whisper, "the proposal? How did you propose?"

"I'm a private man. So I didn't do a spectacle or a show like in the movies. One morning, after we'd spent hours making love, I slipped a five-carat, oval-shaped, Harry Winston engagement ring on your finger. Then we made love once more. After you said yes, of course."

I didn't know why I was testing her like this, tempting her. The logical part of me was screaming for me to abandon this crazy scheme because I knew it was reckless. But I couldn't help myself. And with few hours left on this flight with a king-sized bed just a few feet away, being trapped with this woman that I'd promised not to touch was the very epitome of torture. Sadistic, really.

She shifted in her seat, her fingers trembling slightly as they played with the hem of her shirt. The tension between us crackled in the confined space of the cabin, an unspoken challenge hanging in the air.

I needed to break this pull I felt toward her and shift my focus to something more *controllable*. I reached into the leather briefcase to my left and pulled out a manila envelope. "To ensure there are no misunderstandings, I had my attorneys draw up a contract for the week."

She looked at the envelope, then back at me, her eyes a mix of curiosity and wariness. "A contract? You had your attorneys draw up a contract *for this* ... in less than twenty-four hours?"

"I have an efficient team. This simply outlines our roles, expectations, your compensation and, most importantly, our boundaries."

Her fingers brushed against mine as she took the envelope, the brief touch sending a spark through my veins. "Boundaries, huh?" she asked with a grin.

"Just to keep things professional," I said, my voice sounding more strained than I intended. "We wouldn't want to complicate things, right?"

Timantha opened the envelope and began to read, her eyes scanning the pages. The silence stretched out, thick with unspoken need. Every second felt like an eternity, my resolve weakening with each passing moment.

Finally, she looked up, her eyes locking onto mine. "And what if I don't want to keep things professional?"

My heart raced, but I didn't want her to know the effect she was having on me. Keeping my distance was the only way to stay safe, to keep her safe from me. Because if I let myself get close, if I let her know what she did to me, I'd end up owning her—and she wouldn't even have a choice. *Fuck, I wanted her.*

I leaned in closer and unzipped the jacket of her burgundy jogging suit, revealing more cleavage than the tank top that was underneath. "You are exquisite," I said, gently using the back of my hand to trace a line from her chin, down to her collar, stopping just above her breasts. "So, I don't want you to think that what I am about to say is a rejection of you personally." She shifted in her seat, her breaths heavy.

"This week, these meetings," I continued, "are too important for me to lose focus. And with you, I'd abandon anything important and recklessly bury myself in you. I can't let that happen."

I hadn't had a relationship in five years. I hadn't let a woman this close in what felt like forever. As serious and socially awkward as I was, I was still an insanely possessive man. The moment I let a woman into my life, I wanted to own her completely, and the last time I'd done that, losing her had ruined me so thoroughly that I vowed never to allow anyone that close to me again. Timantha had everything she needed to do it to me once more—ruin me. And truth be told, I wanted to be ruined. I was willing to be utterly and completely destroyed ... *by her.*

Chapter Eight

Timantha

"More wine for you, Ms. Spellman?"

"Yes, Lydia! Thank you!"

I could *really* get used to this.

Will was engrossed in his email or something when I asked, "How much longer do we have on the flight?"

He stopped to glance at his watch. "Three more hours. So you might want to slow down on the wine."

I brushed him off. "Please, I'm ..." A hiccup escaped my lips. "I'm fine," I said unconvincingly.

After the few intense moments we shared, ready to rip each other's clothes off, we both did everything in our power to distract ourselves from the obvious. We asked each other questions to get to know each other better. We ordered food and drinks just to put a third person between us. I even encouraged Will to do some more research on the company he was trying to strike a deal with, just to get his eyes focused on anything else but my breasts.

While Will handled his business, I took care of mine. I sat back in the plush leather seat of the plane, the contract spread out on the tray table before me. My eyes skimmed over the pages, widening at the increasingly ridiculous expectations Will had outlined for our week together. Attend all his high-profile meetings? Check. Maintain strict confidentiality about our arrangement? Check. But the kicker was the ironclad clause about no sex. So he *was* serious about that.

I felt a wave of disappointment wash over me. I couldn't help but glance over at Will with his sharp suit and smoldering gaze. He was undeniably sexy, and the idea of spending an entire week in close proximity to him without exploring that chemistry felt like pure torture. And frankly made no sense.

What was I doing? Who was I kidding? This was the most dangerous and idiotic thing I could have done, and no one even knew where I was. I sent a quick text message to my mom and my best friend, telling them that I was being *"flew'd out"* to meet an international client and then powered down my phone before I could get their panicked responses.

I didn't really know this man. I had no idea if I could trust him. But in the few hours since my abduction, something had shifted. We'd become friends. I liked him. I admired him. And even though he was completely out of my league and out of this world, I found myself enjoying the fantasy we were creating together. I was reveling in this little game of pretending to be his, even if it was just for a fleeting moment. It felt thrilling and dangerously seductive, and I couldn't help but get lost in all of it.

"What kind of work do you do, exactly?" I asked. Because even though I knew what a venture capital firm was in theory, I knew there were nuances to the industry that few people really understood.

"I find companies that are performing below their potential and I provide the founders with money and mentorship to help them turn a profit, thereby helping my firm turn a profit as well."

"Ever made a bad investment?"

"Of course," he replied with a chuckle. "You don't learn what it takes to win if you're afraid to fail. Take losses."

I let out a sardonic breath. "Yeah, but it's easier said than done."

"What is?"

"Taking the risk without being afraid to take the loss. When you grow up poor, you don't have the luxury of taking those kinds of risks. There are no safety nets or trust funds. Things not working out could cost you your life," I said, not really sure why I'd shared that with him. "It's why I've tried to live my life as predictably as possible," I continued.

"Why, because you can control things better?"

I shrugged. "Yeah, pretty much. Things have less of an opportunity to surprise you if you stay prepared. Two steps ahead. *This* is the most adventurous thing I've ever done. I'm normally a pretty boring and strait-laced person."

"Well, technically, *you* didn't do this. I did."

"Yeah, but I was probably going to agree to it anyway. It was going to be the one time in my life where I could say I was taking an adventure. The one time I didn't let fear hold me back."

"I won't pretend to know what that's like growing up the way you did, but I do know what it feels like to be deathly afraid of taking a step toward something better, even if you know the likelihood of things working out in your favor. The fear—"

"Paralyzes you," I finished.

We held each other's gaze for a beat before breaking eye contact. "Do you have an idea for a dream wedding?" he asked, and I had to laugh at that.

"I was *not* expecting that question."

He shrugged. "I figured it's something a woman might ask you this week."

"I used to have an idea, but not anymore."

His curiosity was piqued. "Oh yeah? Why not anymore?"

"Because after having what you thought was your dream wedding, you wake up from the dream realizing the marriage was a nightmare."

"So you've been married before?"

"Yep. Divorced for four years."

"Have you been with anyone since?" he asked.

"In a relationship? No. Of course I've had *situationships,*" I said suggestively, but Will didn't seem to get it.

"What's a situationship?"

I laughed. "A 'friends with benefits' kind of thing."

Awareness fell on his face. "Ahh. I see." His expression darkened, and I saw a mischievous glint in his eyes. "And how long has it been since you've had a *situationship* like that?" he asked.

"A year," I confessed. "What about you?"

"Five years," he shot back. Very quickly and very matter-of-factly.

"Five years!?" I shrieked. "But you're … you're so …"

He raised an eyebrow, a smirk playing on his lips. "So what?"

"Sexy and suave and commanding! You carry yourself like a man who has a different woman in his bed every night! What about the women you're always photographed with?"

"You think I'm sexy?" His voice was a low rumble that sent a lightning bolt of lust straight to my center.

I laughed nervously. "Stop it! You know what I'm saying! How are you *okay* with no sex for five years?" My mind raced, wondering how he managed to maintain his resolve through such an extended dry spell.

"You don't last long in this business without self-control, Timantha," he said, his gaze intense. "And the women you always see me with are props. Nothing more."

I saw the way he watched me. The way he bit his bottom lip every time he peeked at my shirt. He had a decent amount of self-control, alright. But it was fading fast. I could see it all over him. But something about a man being so controlled made me want to corrupt him.

"So you just wander around town, picking up women and sexually frustrating them on your private plane after you've kidnapped them?" I asked, half-joking, half-serious. The man had me on fire.

He unbuckled his seatbelt and got on his knees, his eyes never leaving mine. My chest rose and fell rapidly as I waited to see what he was about to do. I wanted to ask him, but something in his gaze told me to wait.

He inched toward me on his knees, gently opened my legs, and I silently cursed his assistant for removing the pencil skirt I was wearing at the coffee shop. I watched as his hands glided up and down my thighs, his touch sending shivers through me. "I haven't let myself get this close to a woman, close like this, in a long time," he said in a low, breathless voice.

"Why not?" I whispered, though I didn't really care. I was just glad he was this close to me now.

"Because," he whispered, his hands moving from gently caressing my thighs to firmly gripping them from the outside. "I'm possessive. I don't do well with sharing," he breathed, and I could taste the arousal in the air.

"I'm not even sure I want kids because I wouldn't want to share my lady," he continued. This man was an inferno. "A woman like you is dangerous for me, Timantha Spellman."

His words sent a thrill through me. The intensity of his gaze, the way his hands claimed me, made me feel both vulnerable and powerful. His honesty, raw and unfiltered, only added to the magnetic pull between us.

"And what makes me so dangerous?" I breathed.

"Everything," he replied, his eyes darkening with desire. "Your strength, your beauty, the way you challenge me. You make me want things I've tried to deny myself."

His confession was a heady rush, making my pulse quicken. I reached out, my fingers threading through his hair, pulling him closer.

I wet my lips, trying to maintain my composure. This man oozed sex and satisfaction. "And your dates to these events? How do you maintain that stance when you're paying them—me—to be something you clearly need in your life?" I asked, flicking my eyes between his and the steel rod in his pants that had to be torturous. "Why not just fall in love?" I asked, grabbing his tie and attempting to pull his face closer to mine, but he resisted. He was strong. "Why not fall in love with a woman who enjoys being owned? Possessed?" I teased suggestively, and he let out a tortured breath.

His hand trailed a path from my thigh to my stomach, pausing tentatively as he stared deep into my eyes, waiting for permission. I looked at him, willing his hand to continue its exploration as his thumb traced circles around my waist.

"Because falling in love means giving up control," he murmured, his voice a seductive rumble. "And I can't afford to lose control."

I tightened my grip on his tie, a challenging glint in my eyes. "Again, maybe you've just been looking in the wrong places," I whispered, daring him to take the plunge. "Maybe you just haven't found the woman who wouldn't dare consider taking your power away."

His eyes darkened with something more profound and dangerous than the desire I'd seen moments before. His hand resumed its journey, moving up to cup my breast, his thumb brushing over my hardened nipple through the fabric of my top. I gasped, my body arching toward his touch, craving more.

"You're playing a dangerous game, Timantha," he growled, "and I'm not sure you understand the stakes."

"Maybe I do," I whispered back. "Maybe I *want* to play."

I bit my bottom lip as I slid my right hand into my pants and Will stiffened—both in his seat and in his pants. My chest rose and fell with heavy breaths as my hand moved in a circular motion beneath the fabric of my pants.

"Timantha," he warned, but I ignored him, closing my eyes and surrendering to the pleasure as it built.

"So you're saying that," I breathed, and a curse escaped Will's lips.

I was full-on pleasuring myself in mid-air, and there was nothing he could do about it. Well, there was *something*.

"If you had a woman who enticed you with things like this," I said, and I could see the effort it took for him not to claim me right there. But I was toying with him, and he couldn't give in. *Wouldn't* give in.

His hand continued to travel up my stomach, dipping beneath my tank top while I continued tracing wet circles around my needy clit. He grabbed my breast, pulling it out of my bra, and I saw his left hand squeeze his hardened length.

"Fuck, Timantha," He cursed, twirling my nipple in his hand as his eyes bore into me. I didn't stop. I didn't relent as my orgasm built in and around me.

"Do you want me to possess you, Timantha?"

I nodded furiously. "Yes."

I had been touched before, but never like this. Never in a way that lit my entire being on fire. He didn't even have to lay a hand on me; his gaze touched every inch of my body and commanded my soul like an exorcism.

"Shit, Tim," he groaned, dipping his head to put my nipple in his mouth while he stroked himself ever so gently. He was hard, painfully so, but it was clear that he didn't want to give in.

I tilted my head back against the seat and let out a sharp breath. "Shit, yourself!" I moaned, the pressure building.

We heard the curtain open up at the front of the plane, signaling Lydia's approach. Will quickly fixed my clothes and stood from his kneeling position. His erection made me lick my lips.

He took his seat just as Lydia reached us to collect our glasses and plates. "Can I get you anything else, Mr. Huntley? Ms. Spellman?" she asked, her voice polite but her eyes curious.

"No," Will clipped, his tone sharp. Lydia's face revealed that she knew she'd interrupted *something*.

"Finish reviewing the contract, make a list of any modifications you want, then sign the fucking thing," he demanded, his voice thick with authority. In an instant, everything shifted back to business, away from the heated moment we'd just shared.

I nodded, trying to steady my breathing and focus. The intensity of his command was still fresh in my mind, a stark contrast to the passion we'd just experienced. I picked up the contract, the legal jargon blurring slightly as I tried to concentrate.

Will's presence was a constant distraction, his raw, commanding energy filling the space between us. I could still feel the ghost of his touch on my skin, the memory of his breath. Despite the abrupt return to professionalism, the fire he'd ignited in me was far from extinguished.

Chapter Nine

Timantha

I wish I could talk to Tika right now. She was the friend who always advised me to throw caution to the wind because we only lived once. Coincidentally, she was also the one responsible for getting me hooked on dark billionaire romance novels. So if I ended up murdered at the bottom of the ocean, my blood would be on her hands.

My books were the only thing making this farce seem like an adventure. They were why I was acting so out of character. I was a fun person and known to turn it on for my girls in the name of a good time, but that stunt I'd pulled with Will earlier was the type of behavior I usually reserved for a long-term boyfriend. In reality, I'd only opened myself up like that to my ex-husband, and that blew up *royally* in my face.

Typically, I was private about my sexuality. I wasn't a prude; I had just grown accustomed to guarding it because it was usually the first thing men brought up once they'd seen me from behind. Will was so uptight and seemed so unbothered, I just wanted to find a way to get a rise out of him. *And just like Maya Angelou, rise he did!*

I was not expecting him to walk away from me, though. His self-control was something that should be put in a lab and studied. I knew he found me attractive. Besides him telling me as much, his body responded to me whenever he was near me. But for him to be able to do those dirty, seductive things with his tongue to my fingers, and then nonchalantly walk away with a fully erect penis, the man was a freak of nature.

There was an area in the middle of the plane that looked like a living room with a sofa and reclining chairs facing a large, flatscreen TV. After my *performance* for him, I found him sitting there. I sat in one of the chairs opposite him while he typed something furiously on his laptop. "Sorry about that," I said, but he didn't immediately respond.

He grinned but never took his eyes off the screen to meet my gaze. "Did you get what you needed back there?"

I smacked my lips. "No. You stopped me before I could finish."

"I didn't stop you. You could have continued to your heart's content, Timmy. I just wasn't going to join you." He may have seemed unshakable, but I could tell I had an effect on him. He was just really good at hiding it.

"It won't happen again," I said sheepishly, but he shook his head, seemingly brushing it off.

"You can do whatever you like with your body, Timmy." He finally took his eyes away from the computer screen to meet my gaze. "Just try to keep it to yourself next time?"

"What did I tell you about calling me Timmy?"

"You behave, and so will I," he said before returning his attention back to his screen.

The rest of the flight seemed to fly by. I was reading a new release from one of my favorite authors, Christina C. Jones, and I'd reached a sex scene, forcing me to close the book. There was no way I was going to read one of her sexually charged scenes when I had this beautiful man sitting across from me that I could do nothing with.

"I need a shower. Can I use the shower?" I asked, flustered and speaking much faster than I realized.

His eyebrows came together in confusion. "Are you okay?"

"I'm fine." *And horny.* "I'd just like to take a shower before we land. Where are my things?"

Still confused, Will pointed to a compartment that looked like a tiny closet. "Over there. I asked my assistant to pack your leisure wear since I have a stylist coming to meet you once we get settled."

My eyes got big. "A stylist? How did they get my sizes?" Will flashed me a knowing glance. "Never mind," I said once it registered. "I forgot you people are well versed in abduction." Will smirked as I sauntered off to the master bedroom area where the shower was.

I'd only ever flown commercial and never in first class, so transitioning straight from the cramped coach seating of commercial flights to mid-air private luxury was the culture shock of the century. The bathroom looked like it belonged in a five-star hotel, with marble countertops and gold fixtures. The shower even had a spa-like feel with jets designed to massage your senses. I was in heaven, and for the first time, I actually considered marrying Will Huntley as I took in the luxurious space. If I had it my way, I would never fly coach like a peasant again!

I was packing up my belongings, inspecting what all his assistant had packed, when Will came out of the bathroom holding up a container of my haircare products. "You use this?"

"Oh! Devine Luxe! Yes! I can't live without my precious DL!"

"What are the odds? That's the company I want to pitch!"

I stood up straight to meet his gaze. "Pitch for what again?" I asked, my voice laced with an edge of concern.

I fully supported the expansion of Black commerce and wealth, but not at the cost of Black excellence and lives. For far too long, Black hair care products had poisoned our community, with many lawsuits proving that certain companies' products were harmful to us. People usually assumed that Black-owned companies were established simply to create wealth. However, in many cases, companies were founded to create products that were safe for our bodies, hair, and skin when mainstream companies couldn't care less.

It was a cautionary tale. When an independently owned Black hair care company got bought out, the product changed as soon as the ownership did. I didn't want to be part of that kind of change or transaction, no matter how much money it offered. Protecting the integrity and safety of our products was more important than any paycheck to me.

"I know this is none of my business, and it wasn't part of the contract, but would you mind telling me *how* you're going to position Devine Luxe for expansion? How you're going to make it more profitable?"

Will's gaze flashed to a confused one. "What do you mean? What kind of question is that?"

"I mean, do you plan to change anything about the foundation of the company that would make the product subprime or less?"

He fixed me with a stare. "I can't say what I plan to do, Tim. Not before I get into the business' assets and their books. I'm confused as to why it matters."

He closed the distance between us, and I averted my eyes. "It matters because men like you, companies like yours, see businesses like these and think you have what it takes to make it better. When it was perfect the way you found it. With pure intentions of helping the people it was designed to serve."

"Wow. Men like me?" he said, sounding offended.

"You know what I mean, Will. People with profits at the heart of their agendas. I don't want to be part of you destroying a company by diluting it down from everything that makes it good."

"Timantha," he whispered.

He reached for my hand, but I snatched away. "Promise me!" I demanded, but he just stood there with a straight face.

"I'm afraid I can't do that," he said.

"Then I'm not doing this. I won't."

His eyes turned serious. "You signed a contract, Timantha."

"Do you really want to submit a contract to a court of law where I itemized all the ways and places I want you to get me off?" I asked, and he acted as if I'd asked him the weather or time of day.

His jaw tightened. "You did what?"

I shrugged. "You told me to review the contract and add any changes or corrections I wanted made, right?"

His gaze turned dangerous as he punctuated each word of his next question. "What. Did. You. Do?"

I smiled. "What you told me to do! I made a list of changes I wanted added to the contract, Will. How I want you to eat me out on the grounds of the Versailles. How I wanted to be fucked in the Eiffel Tower. How—"

"Timantha. This isn't a joke."

"Says the man who kidnapped me with a smile?"

His face was full of displeasure, but he quickly straightened. He walked back into the bathroom that was adjacent the bedroom, and I watched as he sat my bag of products on the sink.

He calmly walked back into the bedroom, his heavy footsteps matching the pounding inside my chest. Then he brought his hand to my chin to turn my face toward him. "A contract is a contract, Timantha. In order for it to be upheld, the entire contract must be submitted to the courts." He shrugged, feigning indifference. "Your fault for not considering the fact that it would be public record." He tsked. "And just as your little business is getting up and running off the ground."

"Public?" I gulped.

"Yes." He leaned in and whispered in my ear, "All court filings are public record, Timmy. It won't bother me letting the world know how much you want me. They already think I'm a player." He shrugged.

"You tricked me!" I shot back.

"How did I trick you?"

"You kidnapped me!"

"You forgave me. I think it started when you fingered yourself to high heavens. Literally."

"Well! You made me sign the contract under duress, without telling me who the client was!"

"Or perhaps you irresponsibly signed a contract without inquiring about who the client was. Besides, no judge is going to believe that I drew up a contract and you modified it to include *those details* under duress."

"Uggh!" I groaned. "How could I be so stupid!?"

He walked back into the bathroom and brought me my Harry Winston engagement ring that I'd left sitting on the counter before gently placing it on my finger.

"Tim, I think I've deceived you enough for the trip. For a lifetime," he said with a chuckle. "Concealing a detail like this was not my intention. I would have picked your brain about the company much sooner and we could have had a conversation about your concerns."

I searched his face as his voice trailed off and his attention was fixated on the ring he'd just placed on my finger. It was a beautiful diamond, and with the name Harry Winston, the thing had to cost more than my house.

"However," Will continued, "you *did* sign a contract. So regardless of your feelings on the matter, a deal is a deal."

He was right. I had tied myself to this man for the next seven days, and there wasn't a single thing I could do about it. Of course, I could go to the authorities once I arrived in Paris, but I didn't trust how I'd be treated by foreign police. Besides, the money to pay off debt and for my app would mean everything to me. It was just that this new detail added an extra layer of guilt to the entire situation. I didn't like how it was making me feel.

"Will, this isn't who I am. I already felt a way about accepting money for this arrangement. And—"

Will took my hand in his, tracing circles around the diamond on my ring finger. "Tim, I—"

I stopped him, placing my hand on his chest. "And to add insult to injury, I might be helping you cheapen a product that helps so many people. Helps me! Do you know that hair oils help people with alopecia? My mom has it. And here I am, prostituting myself out to help you ruin it all!" I yelled, burying my hand in my face.

Will barked, "Don't you ever call yourself a prostitute in my presence again," he commanded, taking my hand and placing a gentle kiss on it. "Now, I'm sorry that even putting you in this position is making you feel that way about yourself, but it's also why I stipulated no sex. It would do you nor I any good to be

67

caught paying for sex. This isn't about *you,* Timantha. *This* is about business. I offered you money for business, not for your body. *You*, Timantha, are priceless."

I looked at him with fire in my eyes and steel in my spine. "But I also won't be bought. You can't pay me enough to betray a brand I love and who helps so many."

I walked toward the door of the bedroom before turning back to add, "And the moment I get a whiff of you contemplating doing something that will damage this company's reputation for their adoring customers, the deal's off."

"Timantha, what does that mean, the deal is off? Would you say something to Malika Conyers?"

I fixed him with a stare. "Try me and see. I'll do the bare minimum, Will. But don't expect an Oscar worthy performance. That way you can feel free to be the cold, brooding husband, sweet darling. Because that's *exactly* what you'll be getting from me."

Chapter Ten

Will

Well, shit. We were expected to land in Paris in thirty minutes, and it had taken all of eight hours to get Timantha on board with playing my fiancé—only to completely turn her off to the idea and make her flat-out against it. She had to know that I had no idea she used those products. It was all a really strange coincidence. A strange coincidence that I'd seen Timantha, been so taken by her that I ... well, took her ... only to find out that she was the perfect person to be on my arm this week because of her vast knowledge of Malika Conyers and her products. I had to make things right. She was the key to everything going really well or insanely bad.

I found her sitting in the living room area watching an old episode of the Golden Girls. "May I join you?" I asked, gesturing to the seat next to her.

Her eyes remained fixed on the TV screen. "It's your plane. Sit where you like."

I took the seat next to her, ignoring her childish pouting. "You know this wasn't intentional, right? Timantha, I didn't know you used those hair care products."

She turned to look directly at me. "I'm going to ask you something, and I want the absolute truth. If you lie to me, I won't just be your wife this week. I will be your alcoholic wife with the bad wig that you have to keep hidden away from the public."

I squinted my eyes. "Okay."

"Did you choose me because I'm Black?"

"Absolutely not," I clipped. "Timantha, when I first stumbled on your card at the gentleman's club, I assumed you were a man. Curiosity led me to your website with the sole intention of finding a date. But the moment I laid eyes on you, everything changed. You were a vision, captivating and stunning. For all I cared, you could have been the color purple. Your presence was mesmerizing, and I felt an undeniable pull to be close to you, in any way I could."

"Wow," she swooned, not even attempting to hide her grin that was stretched across her face.

"I promise you, I will do everything in my power to keep the foundation and the integrity of the company solvent. But if what I've heard about Malika is true, she wouldn't sign a deal with me that offered her anything other than exactly that."

Her eyes met mine, and then she quickly looked away. "Can I ask you another question?"

"Sure."

"Have you ever been—"

"Yes," I answered, already knowing where she was going.

"How did you know what I was going to ask?"

"Because every Black woman who dates a white guy wants to know if she's being courted or fetishized by him."

70

"Wow, that was direct."

"You should know that about me by now, sweet darling," I teased.

"So, you've had serious relationships with a Black woman before?" she asked. *What was it with this woman and the questions?*

Serious relationships had never been my forte, and I didn't feel like cataloging all my failed attempts. Women were complex, often bewildering, with their desires for flowers and check-in calls. I simply didn't have the time or patience for that, and most women couldn't handle that part of me. They adored the lifestyle I offered but despised the reality of the life I led.

"Serious relationship, no," I replied, hoping that would be the end of it.

"So just sex?"

I wiped a hand over my face. "Yes."

"Why not?"

"Why not what?" I asked in a frustrated tone.

"Why haven't you had serious relationships with Black women? They weren't good enough?"

I let out a sardonic laugh. "No, Timantha. It's because Black women don't really *like* me. Okay?"

"Because you're an asshole?"

"No. Because I'm white," I snapped back.

She shook her head, chuckling. "No. That's not it, bruh."

"What do you mean? How would you know?"

"Because there is an entire TikTok community about white men and Black women. Whether it's about hard wigs and soft lives or Black wives glamming up their white husbands—it's proof that you being white isn't the problem."

"So what do you think it is?"

She turned to face me again. "You're asking me why I think a Black woman would rather sleep with you than date you?"

I shook my head. "Well, not in those words exactly, but yes."

"Because you're an asshole," she said sharply, and I winced at how quickly she arrived at that conclusion again.

"You're not always that way," she continued, her voice softening just a fraction. "But I'd bet anything she didn't feel desired by you in any way other than sexually."

She hit the nail on the head. It didn't matter who the woman was, that was always their observation about me. I was cold, distant, and unconnected. In bed, I was a force of nature, making them feel like they were the center of my universe. But outside the bedroom, it was as if they barely existed to me. I didn't know how to carry the fire I ignited in the bedroom into the rest of our relationship.

She turned to look at me directly, and in that moment, it felt like I was seeing her for the very first time. "Has anyone told you that before? About Black women feeling fetishized?"

"No," I replied, my voice steady, but my heart pounding. "I've spent enough time in boardrooms with despicable men who have devilish intentions and dated enough Black women to have gathered that all on my own."

She shook her head as if understanding was sweeping over her. "I see." She looked appreciative.

Growing up and playing sports, I was always surrounded by a diverse group of friends. We were a tight-knit crew, an unbreakable bond that formed on the playgrounds and sports fields. It didn't matter if they were Black, white, Asian, or any other ethnicity—they were my best friends. My brothers. And those brothers had sisters. Beautiful, captivating sisters who often caught my eye and stirred my young heart. What can I say? My affinity for chocolate never quite went away.

The pilot came over the speaker, letting us know we were preparing to land, and I grabbed Timantha's hand. "I promise you that if you play nice this week, I will make a deal with Malika Conyers that ensures the foundation of not just her brand, but the family and community she's built."

Timantha looked up at me and flashed me the biggest smile. I would love to make her smile like that over and over again. "Deal," she said.

I held her gaze, probably for far too long, then I turned away. But it wasn't quick. I studied her intently, committing every detail of her face to memory before her smile could fade. Her almond-shaped eyes sparkled with an intensity that drew me in, framed by long lashes that cast delicate shadows on her high cheekbones. Her full lips, so inviting and perfectly shaped, hinted at secrets I desperately wanted to uncover.

No other woman had ever captivated me like this, and I didn't know how I was going to keep my hands off her. The thought of her consumed me, and the desire to touch her, to claim her, was almost unbearable.

"Put your seatbelt on. Safety first," I said with a wink. Then I moved away from her and buckled my own seatbelt.

She didn't say anything. She simply leaned back, fastened her seatbelt, and let her head fall against the headrest.

Chapter Eleven

Timantha

"What do you mean, Paris? Texas or California?" my mother asked in an elevated tone.

"Momma, calm down. It's still early in the morning there."

"Don't tell me to calm down! You send me a random email that I barely knew how to open to tell me some man was flying you somewhere? Got my blood pressure up thinking you been sex tracking yourself!"

I shook my head. "It's trafficking, Momma. And I'm fine. I'm safe. I just wanted you to know where I was." She didn't need to know about the sex I was actively trying to seduce this man into having with me.

I cleared my throat, bracing for impact. "And it's Paris, France, Momma."

"France! What in the world is all the way over there that you couldn't order on Amazon?"

We were checking into the Hôtel Étoile d'Or, which I learned meant, "Hotel of the Golden Star," and I'd stopped to call my mother while Will checked us in.

The Hôtel Étoile d'Or was an enigma wrapped in grandeur and mystery. From the moment I stepped through its gilded doors, I felt its history breathing down my neck—a tangible sense of untold stories and secrets whispered behind closed doors. It was the perfect place for a dark romance to unfold.

Marble floors, polished to a mirror sheen, echoed every footstep, each sound amplifying the suspense that hung in the air. Rich, dark woods lined the walls, adorned with intricate carvings and portraits of ancient nobility whose eyes seemed to follow me wherever I went. The air was scented with a mix of aged leather, fresh roses, and a hint of something more elusive—maybe a promise or a warning.

Every corner of the hotel seemed to hold a secret, every shadow a potential revelation. It felt like I had been transported into one of my romance novels, and I couldn't resist the pull to uncover the stories hidden within these walls. I wanted to dive headfirst into the mix of danger and desire that the Hôtel Étoile d'Or seemed to promise. This was a place where passions ran deep and the line between reality and fantasy blurred. The perfect setting for the adventure of a lifetime.

I don't know why I thought my mother would be subdued since it was so early in the morning where she lived. The woman was notorious for being fiery and on ten the moment her feet hit the floor. It didn't matter what day of the week it was or how early in the morning, my momma could make even the devil nervous. Growing up, she used to tell me that there was nothing wrong with making sure your voice was heard.

My mother always encouraged me to be a bit selfish and live a little. She was a huge fan of the author Demetria Lucas, one of the first Black American women she saw documenting her life while traveling and living abroad. It fascinated her. Whenever she wanted me to step out of my comfort zone, she would often shout, "See some world!"—the trademark phrase of the influencer. So, even though I was out of the country and beyond her reach, I could hear the spark of excitement in her voice radiating through the phone. I was finally doing what she always hoped I would—seeing some world.

We were exiting the elevator to the floor where our rooms were, and my mother was still going on about where I was and who I was with. "And what's this man's name?" she asked, and I could tell she was piping up to do *the thing* she did whenever I went on a date with a man she hardly knew.

When I was seventeen, I was already taking college courses. So naturally, I met college guys who wanted to take me out on dates. Until I turned eighteen, Momma had a strict rule that I could only date guys who were one year older than me. And every time someone came to pick me up, she would verify it by asking to see their driver's license. Then, to add insult to injury and deepen my humiliation, she would write down their driver's license number. "In case she comes up missin'," Momma would say with a straight face. I was thirty-four years old and the woman still found opportunities to mother me.

"His name is Will Huntley, Momma," I responded.

Will turned around sharply and mouthed, "She wants to know my name?" I shook nodded in the affirmative.

In trying to clue Will in on what was going on, I nearly missed my mom saying that she wanted to talk to Will. "No, Momma. That's not gonna be necessary. We just landed, and I'm sure Mr. Huntely wants to get settled in and rest. As do I," I said just as we stopped in front of a suite with double doors.

The doors opened, and my mouth dropped open. "Oh, my—"

"What? Is everything okay?" my mother said in a panicked tone.

"Everything is fine, Momma." I laughed. "I just didn't expect such a luxurious um … space," I said, clearing my throat.

I watched as the concierge staff brought our luggage into the room and proceeded to unpack all of our things.

"Well, I'm not gettin' off this phone until I meet the man that whisked my daughter away on some sexy getaway!"

"It's not a sexy getaway, Momma. This is business! You will not be talking to—" I was cut off by Will snatching the phone out of my hand mid-sentence.

"Hey, Momma. Will Huntley here. How you doin'?" Will asked as he casually began chatting it up with my momma!

He was a natural charmer with his muscular physique and panty-melting smile. I could tell he had my mother eating out of the palm of his hand. How could she not?

I watched in horror as he paced the floor and seemed to be taking in instructions that she was handing down. "Oh really, now?" he said, turning to me and raising an eyebrow.

I squinted. "Momma, I swear to God if you are telling him anything embarrassing …" I yelled, but it was pointless. Once the woman started running her mouth, she couldn't be stopped.

Will stopped pacing, and all the humor drained from his face. "You want me to do what?" he asked, his eyebrows raised to the ceiling.

Oh no. She was doing it again. "Will, you do *not* have to do anything she's asking you to do."

Will set the phone down on the desk in the living room area and put the phone on speaker. He took out his wallet, pulled out his driver's license, and then took a picture of it. *He was not seriously doing this!*

"Did it come through, Momma?" he asked.

"It just did, baby!" she said, all flirty and shit.

"Do not call her that! She's *my* momma." Goodness, I sounded like a toddler on the playground.

But when he walked over to me and handed me the phone, I scowled when I saw she'd already hung up. "What did she say?" I asked through gritted teeth.

"Nothing. Just that you snore so I need to check on you at night because you refuse to get tested for sleep apnea."

"I only snore when I drink tequila!" I yelled while following him through the entire suite. "And why did you take the phone? You didn't have to talk to her!"

"It was obvious she wasn't going to leave you alone until you did what she wanted, so I did you a favor."

"Well now she thinks we're a *thing*," I said, pouting.

"It's not the worst thing she could think," he replied, walking into the other bedroom.

He was surveying the space and inspecting the rooms, and it dawned on me that I hadn't taken a moment to really

79

appreciate the space that looked like a 19th century suite fit for royalty. It was a two-bedroom, two-bathroom apartment with a living room and full kitchen. A large picture window overlooked the city, and fresh pink roses were all over the space, giving the room a luxurious aroma. I fell in love with the sheer romance it all invited.

"She also said to only allow you to drink almond milk because you are deathly allergic to cow's milk." *She didn't.* "According to her, one drop of dairy milk and you'll be confined to the bathroom for a week!" *Am I too old to be emancipated?*

My mother was the energetic and chatty type, which was usually sweet and endearing when you were at church or the grocery store. But divulging the private details of my incontinence to my billionaire fake husband had me ready to swim back to Atlanta on foot! *I know that didn't make sense, but that was how much my mother infuriated me!* Why did mothers seem to lose their filters the older they got? All she had to do was introduce herself to Will and be on her way. But no, she had to include a few embarrassing secrets for him as well!

The concierge staff had finished unpacking our things and left after Will came from one of the bedrooms to give them a tip. "The room to your right seems to be set up for women with the vanity and extra closet space, so you can take that one. I'll take the other."

"Thank you. That was thoughtful," I said, and he simply gave me a nod.

Once everything was settled, his demeanor shifted, becoming more serious and businesslike. "I have a few things to take care of, but the stylists will be here in thirty minutes to keep you entertained. I've instructed them to bring several outfit options for dinner, daytime meetings, leisurewear, and formal gatherings, so feel free to indulge. I'll be back by 6 p.m. to pick you up for dinner."

He was headed for the door when I called out, "Anything specific you want to see me in for dinner tonight, sir?" Even though he didn't come to a complete stop, I could tell the question, the way I asked it, had caught him off guard.

He opened the door, then turned to look at me, his gaze slowly scanning my body with such intensity that I felt naked and exposed. The air between us thickened with unspoken tension. "Just choose something that *complements* you," he said, his voice low and commanding. Then, without another word, he turned and walked out the door, leaving me with a flutter of anticipation in my chest and a head full of questions.

Chapter Twelve

Will

"How do you know she's here this week?"

My sister Chloe let out a sigh. "She shared a selfie of herself on social media with a caption saying as much."

"Shit!"

"Calm down! You have your secret weapon with you—"

"Yeah, as long as I keep Timantha away from her. Jessica could blow up this deal and my reputation if she finds out I lied to Malika Conyers about being married!"

Now that we knew Jessica was in Paris, going after the same deal I was, every move she made felt like a calculated strike, a constant reminder that she was out there waiting for her chance to get back at me. I sent a text message to my security staff to schedule a meeting. I needed to find a way to keep tabs on her and track what she was doing while she was here. I needed to keep her away from Timantha.

"Will, there's something else I found out."

I stiffened at the ominous sound in her voice. "What is it?"

"The real reason our major investors want you to make a deal with Malika Conyers."

Oh no. "Just spit it out, Chlo," I muttered through gritted teeth.

"Our numbers don't look good, Will. If we don't make a deal and bring on a business in this product category, we could lose a lot more than our reputation. We could lose everything."

I knew things weren't great for our business, but I hadn't realized just how bad they were. One thing people didn't understand about the venture capital world was that even *we* had people to answer to. The money we invested in small businesses came from various funding sources, and if those investments didn't pay off, those sources could pull their funds. After making a few bad investments—thanks to some overhyped tech bros—our firm was barely treading water.

Striking a deal with Malika Conyers would mean increasing our overhead, but the numbers her business was generating made the investment a no-brainer. Rebranding, expanding, and capturing more market share for her could translate to a thirty percent profit for us. It wouldn't be enough to completely turn things around, but it would be the first step in proving that we weren't dead on arrival.

After running a few errands and making a few calls, I was headed back up to the room to get ready for dinner. There was just one thing I needed to pick up from the front desk. With how everything had gone down with Timantha, I wanted to do something nice for her as a way to thank her for agreeing to my crazy plan.

"Good evening, Mr. Huntley," the front desk clerk said in an elegant French accent.

"Good evening. I was told my delivery has arrived?"

"Yes. One moment while I retrieve it from the safe, monsieur." I surveyed the hotel lobby while she disappeared into the back office area.

Since this was the preferred hotel for this week's summits, the lobby buzzed with people from all over the world. Nervous men and women filled every corner, mingling with potential investors and practicing their elevator pitches. The atmosphere was electric, capturing everything I loved about the business. I couldn't imagine what life would be like without this energy, this drive. In that moment, my resolve to save our company intensified. Failure wasn't an option; I had to ensure we stayed in the game.

The woman returned from the back holding a black bag that held a matching box with a large bow. "Here you are, Mr. Huntley."

"Merci." I nodded before turning to head to the elevators.

While on my way there, Malika Conyers was entering the lobby. "Mr. Huntley!"

"Mrs. Conyers. I see you made it after all!" I said, more excited that I had Timantha here to help me sell this lie than I was to actually see her.

"Yes! We did. My husband Jeff and I worked out a plan to tackle these meetings while one of us has the baby. I'm not the first mom to run a successful business, and I won't be the last," she said, smiling.

I winked. "And it's about time we bring working moms to the forefront and show them how success in these roles looks

84

different for everyone," I quipped, surprised at myself for how calmly I was making idle chit-chat.

"Exactly right," Malika agreed. "Hey! Why don't we grab dinner tonight? Do you all have plans?"

I winced. "I'm sorry, I promised my lady a romantic dinner for her first night in Paris, but we are wide open tomorrow evening. If that works?"

I knew that by turning Malika down this evening, I was running the risk of making her feel unimportant, or even giving another potential investor the opportunity to have dinner with her. But I also knew that Malika valued family over everything, so I took a gamble at allowing her to see my affinity for family in action. I also needed to brief Timantha on all of the events of the week before she met everyone.

My plan worked. "Aww!" Malika swooned, placing her heart over her chest. "I completely understand that! You don't want to go breaking a girl's heart on her first night in Paris, do you?"

"Absolutely not," I said, smiling before saying goodbye and walking to the elevators.

I was grinning the entire time I rode up to our suite on the thirteenth floor. But when I stepped off the elevator and into our suite, what I saw absolutely took my breath away.

Chapter Thirteen

Timantha

"Girl! The airplane had a full bedroom complete with a king-sized bed and a bathroom ensuite!"

"Dannnng! That is some high-falutin Beyonce and Jay-Z rich shit!" Tika yelled into the phone, and we both died laughing.

"Exactly! How is this my life right now?"

"Girl, I don't know, but I need you to savor every minute of it, and don't you dare question anything for another second. You deserve this!"

I shook my head. "I really do, don't I?"

"Yes! And I just Googled this man and … *Tim,* have you seen him? Like, *really* seen him? Because he's fine. Ben Affleck as Batman fine!"

I whisper-yelled into the phone, "I know!"

The stylists had come and gone, and I couldn't wait to call Tika and tell her everything about the trip so far. Since Will wasn't in the room, I called her on Facetime, and she watched me as I tried on various outfits for the week. She nearly lost it when I tried on a one-shoulder, gold, sequined, mermaid gown, gasping out of pure shock at its beauty and intricate detail.

"You look like a princess. No, an Egyptian Goddess!" she said, and it looked like she was fanning tears away from her face.

"Oh, Tika, stop it! You're gonna make my mascara run!"

"You just look so dang gorgeous, T! I want you to bask in this like you are claiming this life of your own, okay?"

I shook my head. "Okay, girl. I will."

I was still on the phone with Tika, hanging up the remaining pieces that the stylists left, when I heard the keycard reader to the suite beep. I stepped out of my room to find Will placing a shiny, black bag on the sofa in the living room. When he heard me enter, he turned around, and the look on his face made my breath hitch.

His eyes widened slightly, and his usual composed expression gave way to raw admiration. His gaze roamed over my body, lingering on the gold, sequined ballgown that hugged my curves perfectly. I could feel the heat of his eyes as they traveled from my neckline to the hem, taking in every shimmering detail. The intensity in his eyes made me feel warm all over, as if his look alone could set my skin on fire.

For a moment, the air between us crackled with charged energy. Neither of us spoke, the silence heavy. I could see the desire flickering in his eyes, matching the rapid beat of my heart. It was as if the world outside ceased to exist, and there was only the two of us, caught in this electrifying moment.

It seemed we kept having those charged and electrifying moments between us, and they showed no signs of slowing down. No signs of being extinguished, either. The fire and lust brewing between us was undeniable, a spellbinding blend of desire and forbidden attraction that neither of us could ignore. Each glance, each accidental touch, only fanned the flames higher. It was a dangerous game we were playing, but in that moment, nothing else mattered except the undeniable heat between us.

"Uhh, Tika? I need to go," I said, hanging up the phone without even looking at her to say goodbye.

I held my arms out and spun around so he could see the entire ensemble. He cleared his throat, wetting his lips for extra moisture. "Timantha, you look … you look like you …" He was struggling to find his words, and it was cute. Endearing. "You look beautiful," is what he finally settled on.

"Thank you," I said with a grin. "Your stylists knew exactly what they were doing. I barely had to ask for anything in my style. It seemed they had exactly the types of pieces I would have already chosen." I took a few steps toward him. "Any idea how their selection was so spot on?"

He turned away from me and went to the bar area of the suite that sat near the large picture window. "My assistant has great taste," he said, but he refused to look me in the eye at this line of questioning.

It was uncanny. Every piece the stylists had seemed like it had been pulled directly from my Pinterest board. All the styles and selections where things I couldn't even afford, but I liked to find inexpensive duplicates to create a bougie chic look for myself. I didn't have to create anything though; it was like they read my mind. I would have to thank that assistant of his.

"Why does it feel like you're running away from me?" I asked, teasing but also somewhat serious.

"I'm not running. I'm just thinking."

I raised an eyebrow. "A beautiful woman graces your presence, and you're *thinking*?"

He ignored my playful comment, his focus shifting to the shiny, black bag on the sofa. With deliberate movements, he pulled out a box and carefully untied the bow, revealing an engraved HW on the lid. When he opened it, my mouth fell open at the sight of the Harry Winston yellow diamond necklace nestled inside.

"Turn around," Will commanded, his voice low and authoritative.

I turned slowly, feeling the heat of his gaze on my back. His fingers brushed against my neck as he fastened the necklace, sending shivers down my spine. When he turned me around to face him, I saw a mix of admiration and tortured longing in his eyes. His gaze lingered on the necklace before tracing my collarbone with a feather-light touch.

Will's strong hand came up to gently encircle my neck, his thumb caressing the delicate skin just above the diamonds. His touch was both possessive and tender, a stark contrast to the turmoil I saw flickering in his eyes.

"You should go look in the mirror," he said, his voice a husky whisper, "at how beautifully you make the diamonds sparkle."

His words were a command, but there was a raw vulnerability in his tone that made my heart ache. I moved to the mirror, feeling his eyes on me every step of the way. As I looked at my reflection, the diamonds indeed sparkled brilliantly, but it was the way Will looked at me that made them truly come alive.

This tension, the forbidden attraction between us, it was all there, shimmering in the space between us. In that moment, I knew we were both playing a dangerous game, one where the stakes were higher than either of us wanted to admit.

Chapter Fourteen

Will

Timantha was absolutely stunning. Every man we passed stopped to stare, and it didn't even matter if they had a woman of their own on their arm. When she asked how the stylists had known exactly what types of pieces to bring that matched her style, I panicked, lying to her and saying that my assistant was responsible for it all. When the truth was, while she was sleeping, I'd gone through her social media profiles and took notes from her photos. Pictures of her out with her girlfriends, at business dinners and conferences—they all informed the selections I'd made for Timantha's wardrobe this week. Including the dress she had on tonight.

When I saw the gold dress in the catalogue the stylists sent over, I knew immediately that Timantha had to wear it. The way the fabric shimmered, the elegance of its cut—it was as if the dress had been crafted with her in mind. As if she could get any more gorgeous, I remembered the perfect piece of jewelry to elevate her look.

While selecting her engagement ring, I'd seen a Harry Winston yellow diamond necklace, and the memory of that specific piece stayed with me. I envisioned it draped around Timantha's neck, enhancing the golden hue of the dress and highlighting the honey tones in her chocolate skin.

Without hesitation, as soon as we touched down, I arranged for the necklace to be delivered from a local showroom. I wanted it to arrive the same day, ensuring that when Timantha stepped into that dress, she would be adorned with the perfect finishing touch—an embodiment of timeless elegance and radiant beauty.

We were waiting for the hostess to take us to our private dining area when I leaned in and whispered in her ear, "No one can keep their eyes off you."

"I think it's because I'm wearing the Rock of Gibraltar around my neck!" she whispered, and I couldn't help but smile.

"You're beautiful. The more you own that, the less you'll deflect whenever a man pays you a compliment or admires you," I said, tracing a gentle hand from her shoulder down to the wrist of her exposed arm. Goosebumps appeared at my touch.

As the hostess led us to our private dining area, I couldn't keep my hands off her, embracing her possessively as men gawked and stared. *Shit. Get it together, Will.* Timantha didn't even seem to notice, smiling and whispering pleasantries to the people we passed. She was the kind of woman who was stunning in every way but completely oblivious to her own magnetism.

I tried to ignore it, but having Timantha on my arm felt right, like the most natural thing in the world. I'd paid women to accompany me to events before, but never for an entire week and never had it felt this good. Never had I felt like I didn't want it to end. Yet, beneath the surface, a storm of conflict brewed within me.

I was essentially using her to save my company, and the guilt gnawed at me with every genuine smile she gave. It was why I needed to do everything in my power to keep my emotions in check and my desires at bay. The line between fantasy and reality was blurring dangerously, and I couldn't afford to lose control. Not now. Not when everything was at stake. Seeing the way her every curve was accentuated by the fabric of her dress, I probably should have chosen a different one.

"So," I said, taking a sip from the glass of water that sat in front of me. "First night in Paris. What do you think so far?" I asked, and Timantha's face lit up with immediately excitement.

"It's everything," she said, beaming. "It's not a big city of lights like you see in the movies, but I'm blown away by the charm and sense of romance of it all."

I didn't take Timantha for a hopeless romantic; she seemed too Type A too allow herself to be swept away by love. "So you're a romantic," I commented.

"And you're a cynic, I gather?" she asked, teasing.

"I'm not a cynic. I'm just more practical than most."

"I get that. And if you were to ask my friends, they'd say I'm too predictable to be a romantic. And ordinarily, they'd be right," she said, her voice softening. "But being here with you? I'm allowing myself to be spontaneous. Reckless, even." Her eyes sparkled with a hint of mischief, the kind that promised unexpected adventures and whispered secrets under moonlit skies.

The hotel had private dining quarters for those who had the penthouse suites. It was designed for celebrities or important guests who wanted to dine with a sense of privacy. I clearly didn't think this through because now I was in yet another confined space with Timantha. The low lighting accentuated her features, making her look even more irresistible.

The soft glow highlighted the curve of her neck, the way her dress clung to her figure, and the sparkle of the necklace I had given her. My thoughts were a chaotic mix of desire and restraint, fighting the urge to reach out and touch her.

Just as I was losing myself in the sight of her, our waitress approached our table, breaking the spell. She smiled politely, presenting us with the evening's specials in a melodic, French accent.

"Bonsoir, monsieur et madame. Our specials tonight include a tender filet mignon with truffle butter, a delicate sea bass in a citrus reduction, and a rich, velvety chocolate soufflé for dessert."

I tried to focus on anything else, but my thoughts kept drifting back to her, to the softness of her skin, the way her lips curved into a smile that lit up the room.

Since Timantha had steak aboard the plane, she chose to order the sea bass while I ordered the filet. I added a bottle of their 2006 Château Petrus Bordeaux because I was absolutely trying to impress her.

Timantha leaned across the table and whispered, "That's a four-thousand-dollar bottle of wine! Are you sure?"

I grinned. "It's actually five thousand. And yes, I'm sure. It's my wife's first night in Paris—I have to show her a good time, right?" That made her blush.

It was refreshing to experience Timantha this way. Most of the women I dated couldn't wait to find opportunities to spend my money. Timantha, on the other hand, seemed more conscious about it, and I couldn't help but recall our conversation about how she grew up with no money. Her cautious and safe approach to finances was something I hadn't really seen before.

It was refreshing but also disheartening that I didn't have people in my life who could relate to Timantha's experiences. Her grounded perspective highlighted a gap in my own social circle. The only way I would have even known to appreciate her outlook was by simply listening to her, and in doing so, I found myself drawn to her even more.

We were finishing our plates when Timantha asked, "How many women have you brought to Paris?"

I squinted. "Are we really doing this again?"

"Doing what? I just asked a question."

"I've known you for all of twenty-four hours, and even *I know* that Timantha Spellman doesn't *just* ask a question. You're fishing for something," I said, pouring another glass of wine for both of us.

"You'd better slow down with that wine before I get you drunk and have my way with you," she replied with a sly smile. The look in her eyes told me that all I had to do was grant her permission, and her joke would easily become a guarantee.

Despite my resolve to not sleep with her, she continued to test me. Between her flirtatious banter and downright sinful glances, I didn't know how much longer I could take the temptation.

"Unfortunately for you," I responded in a low growl, "I'm not a man who can be dominated or easily taken advantage of, Timmy. It'll take more than this wine for me to fall victim to your advances."

A glint of challenge flickered in her eyes. "We'll see," she said, raising her glass to take another sip of wine, her tongue slowly licking the area where a drop had escaped her lips.

"Are you like this all the time? Insatiable?" I asked, my voice thick with desire.

"Only when I've been dropped in the middle of a billionaire romance novel with a man who looks like ... *you*."

I raised an eyebrow. "I've heard you mention a billionaire romance novel a few times now and, most recently, while you were on the phone. Is that really a genre?"

"A subgenre, but yes. It's absolutely a thing, which is why I had such a hard time believing this—you—were real. Stuff like this only happens in the books I bury myself in, never in real life." She lit up as soon as she started speaking about her books, her energy infectious.

"I still can't wrap my mind around you being into romance novels. Even as a matchmaker, you don't strike me as the type."

"Oh yeah? And what type of person do I strike you as?"

"Someone practical. Aware. That's the reason I thought you finally agreed to this week. It made sense."

"Two things can be true," she said in a breathy voice, her eyes locked on mine. "Smutty romance just happens to be my guilty pleasure."

I smirked, leaning in just a fraction closer. "Smutty romance?"

"Yeah!" Her voice was a mix of excitement and teasing. "You know, there's always a happily ever after, but there are also some steamy—and sometimes downright dirty—sex scenes that would make your grandmother burn her bra in protest."

I laughed, the sound of a low rumble in the intimate space between us, but quickly resumed my inquiry, unable to resist pushing further. "Is that the part that gives you pleasure? The smut? The dirty stuff?"

Her eyes darkened, a spark of challenge in them. "Why do I have to choose? Why can't I like it all?"

The flirtation between us was getting dangerous, a palpable heat building in the small distance that separated our bodies. "Do you have a favorite story or scene?" I asked, my voice low, almost a whisper. I was torturing myself with that question, but I needed to know, needed to dive deeper into her fantasies.

She bit her lip, her gaze dropping to my mouth for a heartbeat before meeting my eyes again. "There are several," she began, her voice husky, laden with unspoken desire. "Scenes where the tension builds so high, you think they might just combust from the sheer need. It's raw, intense, and when they finally give in ... it's explosive. *I explode*," she teased.

My breath caught, the vivid imagery she painted igniting something primal within me. The air between us crackled with electricity, and I knew, without a doubt, that this conversation was about to push us past the point of no return.

"There's one book," she continues, "where a woman begins a tawdry online relationship with a man she *thinks* lives across the globe."

"This doesn't sound smutty," I quipped.

She ignored my observation and continued, "They're both busy with their own respective lives, too busy for traditional relationships. So they meet up once a week for anonymous, spontaneous cyber encounters."

"Interesting ..." I muse, my curiosity piqued.

"But when she suffers an attack, she finds out that the mysterious man she's been pleasuring herself with from miles away actually lives in her same city."

"So there's mystery smut too?"

"There is smut for some of everything and everyone."

"But you prefer mystery? The intrigue? The danger?"

"And the adventure," she confirmed. "You asked if I'm normally insatiable like this, and the answer is no. But there's something about the allure of this city and in it's environment ... it makes me want to come alive and open myself up to *all of it*."

I hung on every word she was saying, watching her mouth move and her full lips curve with every smile. I reached across the table and caressed her hand.

"So no one's ever *opened* you up before?" I asked suggestively. But just as I asked that, a startling realization hit me—Timantha wasn't wearing a bra.

Her nipples were faintly visible through the fabric of her dress, and the knowledge sent a jolt of desire through me. The room seemed to shrink around us as I noticed the circular shapes that had formed at the tips of both breasts. It wasn't just the outline of her nipples; there was something else hard and round beneath the fabric, framing each peak.

I leaned in, my thumb tracing gentle circles on her wrist, and I could feel her pulse quicken beneath my touch. "Timantha," I murmured, my voice low and strained, "are your nipples pierced?"

Her breath hitched slightly, and our eyes locked. She bit her bottom lip and glanced down at her breasts, the evidence of both her arousal and her piercings on full display. The heat that blazed between us was undeniable, an insatiable burn that was overtaking my body. The stakes were higher than ever, but I was ready to take the plunge, consequences be damned.

She leaned in, allowing her cleavage to spill onto the table. "Do you like that, Will?" she breathed, and suddenly there were no words to describe the strength of the hardness that was threatening to rip through my pants.

"Timantha," I warned, "this is a really terrible idea."

"What is?" she whispered.

We were seated at a booth, and without warning, I rounded the table until I was face to face with her. For the first time since meeting her—and the thousandth time since thinking about it—I captured her mouth and claimed her. I kissed her intensely, the way a man kisses a woman he's been craving for years, as if I'd been starving all this time.

Our connection was electric, and I felt the heat of her lips ignite something deep within me. I broke the kiss before it consumed us entirely, my breath ragged as I took her face in my palms. I looked deep into her eyes, feeling the same longing mirrored in her gaze, and whispered, "Everything. All of it." And

99

I kissed her once more. Something snapped inside, and I couldn't wait to get her to our room.

We left our private dining area and walked to the elevator in silence, but the unspoken truths between us could fill an arena. Whatever began in our private dining area had followed us into the hallways of this exotic hotel and threatened to shatter everything we had planned. And still, I couldn't stop it if I tried.

Chapter Fifteen

Timantha

There was an electric magnetism that flowed between me and Will, like molten lava coursing just beneath the surface. As we exited the dining area of the hotel, my vision was fixated on getting to the elevators as quickly as possible. Every time I felt his hand touch the small of my back, my ache for him intensified.

All I could think about were the scenes I'd read in my romance novels, the ones I'd meticulously transcribed into my journals. When Will asked if I had a favorite spicy scene from my books, I was too embarrassed to tell him there had to be at least twenty, and I knew them all by memory. If there was ever a steamy scene that got my heart racing, I wrote it down verbatim, preserving it for a future partner who could bring those fantasies to life. What I wouldn't give to have that journal with me now. There were so many positions, so many sultry scenarios, that I would kill to try out on this man. The thought of reenacting those passionate moments with Will had my body throbbing with need.

"Mr. Huntley! We keep running into each other!" I heard from behind us just as the elevator car had reached us. *Fuck me.*

Will and I turned to see a striking woman with her husband and baby, the picture of Black love. I felt Will's grip around my waist tighten, but it felt different from the way he held me just moments before. It felt like he was holding onto me to steady him.

"Malika Conyers," he said, his voice steady. "We do, indeed." It was weird. Suddenly Will seemed nervous and unsure of himself.

We stood there for what felt like minutes, and I smiled at Will like an idiot, trying to use some form of telepathy to get him to snap out of whatever was happening with him at that moment.

Extending her hand, Malika asked, "And this must be the lovely wife?"

And since Will was nearly in a trance, I spoke up. "Yes! I am Will's wife, Timantha Spell—"

Will cut in, "Timantha Huntley," he said, correcting me. "It seems my beautiful wife is still getting used to the name change," he said, smiling. Finally, he was back.

I blushed. "You'll have to forgive me. It all is still very new to me."

Will laughed. "Actually, I was only just recently able to convince this one to take my last name." He shrugged. "What can I say? I married an independent woman," Will said jokingly, and we all joined in the laughter.

And just like that, Will had relaxed, easing back into character. At that moment, he didn't seem like a man plagued by social anxiety at all. Instead, he'd snapped back into the man he projected to the world. Confident and self-assured—which was exactly how I saw him.

As Will and Malika finalized dinner plans for the next evening, I noticed Malika watching me, studying me from the corner of her eye. Meanwhile, her husband stood off to the side with their baby, his demeanor much more guarded. There was something in his eyes that hinted at distrust toward Will.

Malika's gaze drifted to my neck. "That necklace shines almost as bright as you," she remarked, and I blushed at the compliment.

"Thank you! It was a gift from this one here," I said, stepping toward Will and leaning into him closer.

"Smart man," she said before turning to her husband to see that he appeared less than enthused about her little detour to speak to us.

Turning back to us, she said, "Well, we won't keep you! We're really looking forward to getting to know you both better!" she exclaimed, but she probably should have clued her husband in on that fact.

"Likewise!" Will shot back before pressing the button to call the elevator again while Malika and her husband glided off to the dining area.

I turned to Will, searching his gaze for answers. "You want to tell me what that was?" I asked, squeezing his hand gently. I didn't want him to feel embarrassed or ashamed of what had just happened.

He pressed the elevator button again, forcefully trying to will it to return to the lobby. "What do you mean?"

"Will, I didn't just imagine that. When you first saw Malika Conyers, you sort of froze." I stepped closer to him and placed a soft hand on his shoulder. "Is that what happens sometimes? With the social anxiety?" He didn't respond. He simply grabbed my hand and guided me into the elevator car as the doors opened.

When we stepped onto the elevator, the passion between us seemed to reignite instantly, wrapping us in an intimate cocoon. Where Will had just been stiff and unsure with Malika Conyers, he now exuded a quiet, commanding presence. The air was thick with unspoken tension as we stood together, waiting for the elevator to reach the thirteenth floor. So far, we'd only made it to the third.

He was standing behind me. The only sound in the confined space was our heavy breaths, each one laden with anticipation and unvoiced desires. I wanted to try to probe more, to make him feel safe with him so he'd open up about the demons he was fighting. But I couldn't bring myself to break the tension. His energy was so intoxicating, it was almost unbearable, an invisible force pulling me toward him.

"You're standing too close," I whispered, my voice barely audible over the pounding of my heart. "I can't think. I can't breathe when you're this close." But he didn't care. He stepped even closer, the heat of his body pressing against mine, sending shivers across my senses.

"What are you thinking about?" he asked, his voice a low and husky rumble that made my knees weak. "What are you *trying* to think about?"

I wet my lips, sheer embarrassment washing over me at the idea of voicing the sinful thoughts racing through my mind. I wanted him to give in to me, to open up to me. But he wasn't the kind of man who unburdened himself to just anyone. He wasn't the kind of man who let a woman see his weaknesses. And if my instincts were right, he was using this moment to regain control of the situation. Of his emotions. Of me.

His breath was hot against my ear as he waited for my answer, the tension between us crackling like a live wire. In that confined space, every touch, every glance, felt magnified; the anticipation was almost too much to bear.

"You," I whispered, and Will took another step closer. By then, we had reached the sixth floor.

The elevator was one of those older models, with metal gates that opened and closed for safety. It moved slowly, inching up each floor, and I silently thanked the heavens for this brief reprieve before we reached our hotel room. I knew that as soon as we made it to our suite, we'd be ravenous, our desire consuming us. But here, in this moment between time and space, I wanted to savor every second of him—his scent, his slow breaths, the rich timbre of his voice. I wanted to capture this feeling and never let it go.

Will took another step closer, and I felt the unmistakable evidence of his arousal pressing against my back, sending puddles to my panties. His arm snaked around me, and with a delicate yet commanding touch, he used his thumb to part my lips, his fingers gripping my neck gently but firmly.

"What about me, Tim? What do you think about when you think of me?" he asked. *Eighth floor.*

Each floor we ascended felt like an eternity, but I cherished every second, every whisper of his breath against my skin, every pulse of desire that echoed between us. I wanted to be lost in this moment forever, to drown in the heat and promise of this night.

"What do I think about?" I managed to say, my voice trembling with anticipation. "I think about your touch, how you might taste, the way you make me feel alive just being near you." His grip tightened slightly, and I could feel his smile against my ear.

I watched him disappear as he knelt down, his movements deliberate and confident. With a swift, practiced motion, he slid his hand beneath my floor-length dress, his fingers expertly navigating the fabric. Within seconds, I felt his touch begin its tantalizing journey, tracing a slow, deliberate path from my ankle, up the back of my calf, then around to the sensitive insides of my thigh. Until—"Ah! Shit!" The words slipped out of my mouth as his fingers reached my clit, and I erupted at the initial sensation of his touch.

My breath hitched, my knees nearly buckling under the intensity of his caress. Every nerve ending seemed to awaken, every inch of my skin hypersensitive to his touch. His fingers moved with precision, eliciting a symphony of sensations that left me breathless and yearning for more.

I bit my lip, trying to stifle the moans that threatened to escape, but it was futile. The pleasure was overwhelming, a relentless wave that crashed over me, leaving me gasping for breath. I could feel the heat building, the tension coiling tight within me, ready to snap.

"Will," I breathed, my voice a desperate whisper. His name was both a plea and a surrender to the exquisite torment he was inflicting on me. He looked up, his eyes dark and filled with a hunger that mirrored my own.

The metal in the elevator car created the illusion of a mirror. When Will stood up, his hand still buried deep inside me while my dress flowed around us, the metal reflected our heated, entwined bodies back at us. Our eyes locked as Will shamelessly traced circles around my clit, his fingers slick with my arousal. It was the sexiest thing I'd ever experienced—the sight of us together, the intensity in his gaze, and the way his touch made me feel while his eyes bore into mine, never losing focus.

I brought my left arm around his neck, pulling him closer, needing his support as my knees threatened to buckle under the weight of the pleasure he was giving me. My breaths came in ragged gasps, each one matching the rhythm of his hands. I opened my legs wider, granting him even more access, craving the deeper connection, the deeper sensation.

His eyes darkened, a satisfied smile playing on his lips as he watched me lose myself in the moment. The reflection in the metal walls showed every detail, every twitch of my muscles, every flutter of my lashes, the way my mouth fell open in silent cries of ecstasy.

"God, you're beautiful," he murmured, his voice a rough whisper that sent a fresh wave of arousal through me. His free hand gripped my hip, steadying me as he continued his relentless assault on my senses. The elevator continued its slow ascent, each second stretched out, a torturous yet delicious eternity.

We finally reached the thirteenth floor, but I wasn't ready for this moment to end. Will had his security detail positioned up and down the hallways of our floor, and I didn't want them to see the brazen need in my expression. With a desperate need for more, I pressed the button to close the doors and pulled the emergency lever, halting the elevator in place for a few precious moments longer.

With a wicked smile, Will pushed me forward, brushing my hair over my shoulder. My hands instinctively reached out, pressing against the elevator doors to steady myself. I gasped as first one finger, then two, slid inside me, his movements deliberate and teasing. His lips and tongue traced a searing path along my back, licking and biting, sending shivers down my spine. "Shhhhit! Will! I'm … coming!" I cried out, the intensity of his touch overwhelming.

"That's it, sweet girl," he whispered, his voice a husky caress in my ear.

I didn't care who heard us. The thought of security cameras recording our every move only heightened the thrill. This man was giving me the best minutes of pleasure I'd ever experienced, and I was completely lost in the sensation, in the raw, unbridled passion of the moment.

My world narrowed to the feel of his fingers, the heat of his breath on my skin, and the sound of his whispered encouragement. Each plunge sent waves of ecstasy rippling through me, my body responding to him with a need that was almost primal. His fingers moved faster, more insistent, driving me higher and higher. I clung to him, my nails digging into his thigh from behind me, needing him to hold me together as I unraveled.

Time seemed to blur, and the tension coiled tighter and tighter within me, until finally, I exploded around him. My cries echoed in the small space, and I didn't care one bit. My orgasm was a shattering release, pure and powerful, leaving me trembling and spent.

Will held me close, his fingers still inside me, grounding me as I came down from the high. The elevator remained still, a silent witness to our passion. I threw my head back against his chest, feeling the solid strength of him, and he gently let the skirt of my dress fall back to the floor.

He pulled me tightly against him, his left hand gripping my neck in a possessive yet tender hold. With a slow, deliberate motion, he took the two fingers he'd just withdrawn from me and brought them to my lips. I parted them, tasting my own essence as he watched through the reflective metal of the elevator, the intimacy of the act making my heart race.

With a final, lingering touch, he pressed the button to release the emergency hold, and the elevator doors slid open. The cool air of the hallway was a stark contrast to the heat that had built between us. I knew that as soon as we stepped out, the night would continue, filled with the promise of more shared moments, more stolen touches, more breathless encounters.

We walked in silence to our suite, the anticipation thrumming between us like a live wire. But as soon as we entered, Will turned to walk toward his separate room, his entire mood and demeanor shifting as if what we'd just shared was all in my mind.

"Goodnight, Timantha," he said, his voice steady and calm. Without another word, he closed his bedroom door behind him.

As I slowly made my way to my own room, a myriad of emotions washed over me—confusion, longing, and a lingering desire that refused to be quelled. And as I settled into my bed, I couldn't help but wonder what tomorrow would bring. What this all meant. But I also had to ask myself, *What would my favorite FMC do in this situation?*

Chapter Sixteen

Will

Taking Timantha in the elevator was the most reckless and idiotic thing I could have done. But damn, it was sexy. Watching her handle Malika Conyers with such effortless grace, slipping into the role of my wife as if she'd been born for it, something inside me shifted. She was able to sense that I needed her, and in that moment, I was just grateful to have her by my side. So grateful that I wanted to thank her. I wanted to thank her long, hard, and slow.

But with the need to maintain some distance, I expressed my gratitude in the only way I knew how ... with just enough to give her what she needed. If I'd had it my way, if I had *her* my way, I wouldn't have stopped. I would've carried her into our suite and taken her everywhere, until she couldn't walk for days. Which was exactly why I *had* to pull back before things went too far.

Timantha was getting too close. She'd witnessed a moment of an anxiety attack, and even though it was mild, she noticed. I didn't like that she was close enough, aware enough, to see into me that way. It had happened dozens of times before, and most women didn't pay attention to me until it was time to take out my wallet. So they certainly didn't catch me during the times when my anxiety got the best of me. But Timantha did. She saw me.

My security detail was always on alert, but I made sure they were especially on guard since I'd learned that Jessica

Lucas would be snooping around. I hated that as soon as it seemed like things were looking up, something else got in the way to knock me off my game.

I wasn't worried about Jessica stealing my opportunity with Malika Conyers. What concerned me more was her potential to destroy my reputation. I was confident that our firm was superior and fully capable of taking Malika's company where she wanted it to go. And, thanks to Timantha, I knew we could do it while preserving the foundation of her company and the community she'd built.

I had four days to convince Malika, and I had to make sure Timantha was on her A game. After last night, after leaving things the way I did, I wasn't sure how she'd respond to me.

There was a knock on the door, and I set my coffee and laptop down to go open it. "Room service for Monsieur Willow Huntley?"

Opening the door wider to let the butler in, I said, "Yes. Just set it by the window next to the bar cart, please?" I pulled out my wallet and tipped the gentleman before he closed the door and left.

No sooner than the front door closed, the door to Timantha's room opened. I wasn't particularly excited to face her, but I'd hoped the obnoxious breakfast spread I'd ordered would help smooth things over after the night before. I wasn't proud of myself, and it wasn't my intention to make her feel rejected. But the pain of what would inevitably happen after this was all over was also why I had to shut it down. I didn't trust myself to let her go once it was all over.

A week. That's all we had. And I knew that once the week was over, Timantha would have no reason to stay with me. After that week, she'd have everything she needed to begin the life she'd always dreamed of. And after that week, I'd likely revert back to the man everyone always left. Everything about how the week would play out and how it would end was inevitable.

I turned around and realized I hadn't yet seen what Timantha wore to bed. *What ... the ...?* "Did ... did my assistant pack that for you?" I asked, my eyebrows raised to the ceiling.

She looked down as if she was confused at what I was talking about. "Oh this? No," she said, nonchalantly shaking her head. "Your assistant had some sweats and an oversized t-shirt for me to sleep in, but that little room was too stuffy for all that! So I found some scissors and cut the shirt and pants into this cute little short and crop top set." She stretched her arms above her head, feigning a yawn, and I saw skin from her breasts peek beneath the fabric of her shirt. "This feels so much better!" she said, smiling.

She was definitely doing it on purpose, flaunting her curves like she knew exactly the effect it had on me. And it was working. Those weren't just cut-off sweatpants—she might as well have been wearing panties. If she lifted her arms any higher, I'd catch a glimpse of her nipples.

Averting my gaze, I attempted to ignore the little show she was putting on. "I didn't know what you'd like for breakfast, so I ordered some of everything."

"Thanks!" she said, hopping to the coffee pot to pour herself a cup. I watched as she added two creams but no sugars before she sat next to me on the sofa. *Did she have to be this close?* "So, what's on the agenda today?" She smelled like lemons and lilacs.

I tried to inch over on the sofa—away from her—without her noticing. "I have a lunch meeting with a potential client, and you and I have dinner with Malika and her husband."

Her eyebrows knitted together. "What am I supposed to do during the day?"

"Take a tour, go shopping ... your per diem is a thousand a day."

"Per diem? Did I miss that in the contract?"

No, but I feel guilty for rejecting you, and I'm trying to purchase your favor. "No. I just realized you didn't plan for this with your bank, and I figured it would be a hassle trying to get your cards to work here."

"Oh!" She shrugged. "That was thoughtful."

She sat beside me on the sofa with her legs crossed while she scrolled her phone and ... how could she consider those things shorts?

"Malika Conyers seemed really taken with me last night," she said, sucking icing or frosting from her fingers. She was a cruel woman. "I think you should give me a bonus for what a fabulous job I'm doing as your fake wife!" she teased, and I bit my bottom lip when she bent over to pick up a crumb she'd dropped from the muffin she was eating.

"And that baby!" she continued. "I just love me a chocolate baby with some chubby cheeks!"

"You like kids?"

"Oh no! God, I hate them," she said, shivering, and I smirked at the unconventional confession.

"Most women your age are pointing at biological clocks right now. Why are you so different?"

She shrugged. "I enjoy my freedom. I enjoy being debt free. And as much as my friends with children love their kids, I've seen them all struggle with the financial and emotional weights that children can be for mothers. I'm just not sure if that journey is for me." She took a sip of her coffee, and I stiffened at the sound of her moaning from the taste.

I enjoyed getting to know her during these moments, and the more she revealed, the more I wanted to know. The more she opened up, the more I found myself craving her presence. Her strength, her vulnerability, the way she saw the world—it was intoxicating. Each piece of her story, every little detail she shared, drew me in deeper, ensnaring me in a web of fascination and longing. And I hated what it was doing to me.

I cleared my throat, shifting in my seat. "Was there … is there anything that you wanted to do while you were here?"

She stopped scrolling the social media app and flashed me the wickedest grin. "Besides you?"

"Timantha, I—"

She sighed and smiled before returning her attention to her phone. "I already know what you're about to say, and I'd love it if you didn't mention it, Willow Huntley."

I narrowed my gaze. "How'd you know my full name?"

"I heard the butler say it when he came in. Did your parents have a thing for the movie *Willow* with the little man?"

I snickered. "They did, actually. Was *your* father's name Timothy?"

She laughed. "It was. Touche!"

"So, Tim. About last night—"

She cut me off. "Are you into the whole S&M thing? Is that why you talked about owning me and stuff on the plane? Why you only give me *some of* you … so you can maintain some semblance of control?"

"No," I said, rolling my eyes. I was intending on apologizing, but her question caught me off guard.

"No to S&M, or no that isn't why you talked about owning me?"

I was into S&M, but she didn't need to know that. Women always pretended to be freaked out by the idea, but as soon as they learned about that culture and what it entailed, they lit up like a Christmas tree, all suddenly curious about how they might enjoy it. The mention of it was the perfect aphrodisiac.

I picked up S&M as a way to harness my power and control. When you suffer from something that leaves you powerless to your own body, you look for ways to compensate for what's been stolen from you. That's what S&M did for me. Whenever I felt out of control, I turned into an altered version of myself and would allow myself to claim, rule, and ruin at my will.

It wasn't just a pastime or a curiosity—it was a lifeline. Each session, each moment of domination, was a reclamation of the power that had been ripped from me. I became someone else entirely, someone strong and unyielding, a force to be reckoned with. The ropes, the commands, the absolute surrender of another person beneath me—they were more than just acts. They were rituals of my own empowerment, a way to rewrite the narrative that my anxiety had tried to dictate.

I let out a harsh breath. "Look, Tim. Last night was—"

"Amazing," she breathed, cutting into my righteous stance. "And I wish you would have fully given in to me," she whispered, and for a moment I thought her tone was innocent. "And if you *were* into S&M," she continued, "I would have allowed myself to be dominated by you, Will Huntley."

She had no idea what she was asking for. No idea what she was playing with, attempting to summon that side of me. In those moments, I was invincible. Every whip crack, every submissive plea for mercy, was a testament to my control, a declaration that I would never again be at the mercy of my own fears. The world might see it as deviant, but for me, it was salvation. It was the balance I craved, the antidote to the helplessness that sometimes threatened to overwhelm me. I had never needed that balance as much as I did when in the presence of Timantha Spellman.

My eyes locked on hers, and where I expected to see seduction in her gaze, I saw longing. I took her phone from her and placed it on the coffee table that sat in front of us. Then I leaned over to grab her arm, guiding her from the sofa to my lap.

She straddled me, and I brought her ear to my lips. "Don't think for a second I didn't want to. Don't think for one moment that last night was about rejecting you," I confessed, stroking her back softly.

I didn't know why I kept doing that—pulling her in and then pushing her away. My behavior mirrored the storm of conflict brewing in my mind. When she was close, I had to touch her. As soon as I caught a whiff of her scent or a glimpse into her eyes, she became the object of my every thought and affection. But the closer she got, the more I felt the urge to pull away.

She pulled back and met my gaze. "I know. It was about control," she said, her stare never relenting.

I stared at her a few seconds too long because, suddenly, the closeness was too uncomfortable. So I picked up her petite frame and moved her back to her spot on the couch. I got up to go rinse my coffee cup, trying to put some distance between us, but she followed me.

"Why are you so hot and cold all the time? Why bring me on a sexy getaway and not offer me the *full* experience? You tell me not to refer to myself as a prostitute, but after last night—"

"Timantha, that's enough," I warned, but she kept coming at me.

"I just think it's funny how you have all this money and all this clout, but you spend it on meaningless encounters and would rather *pay* women to provide you comfort, when they could never see you or know you! I don't think you're against relationships or love. I feel like you *want* to stay hidden as some sort of weird emotional security blanket."

She was hurt. Deep down, her heart was aching, and she lashed out in pain. But she needed to stop testing me like this.

117

She was standing behind me, and I turned so swiftly, she halted mid-sentence, her words hanging in the air like fragile glass. I stalked toward her with a predatory grace, watching as she instinctively retreated, not stopping until her back pressed against the wall.

Her chest heaved with ragged breaths, her panic evident in the wild rise and fall. Her eyes, wide and searching, locked onto mine, desperately trying to decipher my next move. The room seemed to shrink, the air thick with unspoken words and raw emotion. Every muscle in her body tensed, waiting, bracing for what was to come.

"Timantha, whatever my reasoning for keeping my distance ..." I stopped for a moment, unsure of what I wanted to reveal just then. "You're not being paid to diagnose or psychoanalyze me. You're being paid to help me close this deal. Now, would you please stop with all the childish questions and go put some clothes on!" I muttered through gritted teeth, my heart breaking at the deflated look in her eyes.

I needed to be harsh with her. I needed to deter any ideas she had of love, romance, or happily ever after. Even if it killed me to see what it did to her.

As I towered over her, the tortured desire in my chest warred with the dominance and control I used as a shield. I wanted her, craved her more than I cared to admit, but letting her in meant exposing parts of myself I wasn't ready to face. The raw vulnerability she showed chipped away at my resolve, but I forced myself to stay firm.

"You need to understand something," I said, my voice low and commanding. "I need to maintain control of this situation. I *need* to maintain control of what happens between us.

If you can't respect that, then I can arrange for you to go home, and this ends here and now." I said it as if she came here of her own free will. But something told me that she wanted to be here just as much as I needed her to be.

She swallowed hard, the defiance in her eyes dimming slightly as she nodded. But the fire was still there, simmering beneath the surface, and I knew this wasn't over. Not by a long shot.

I turned away, my heart pounding with the effort it took to walk back to the sink. The distance I'd put between us was a temporary fix, a band-aid over a wound that was already festering. And I had a feeling Timantha wasn't going to let it heal anytime soon.

Chapter Seventeen

Timantha

"So how did the two of you meet?" Malika asked. We were just seated for dinner and had placed our orders when she asked the one question everyone always asked a newlywed couple. Thankfully, we'd practiced this one.

I was getting ready to answer when, surprisingly, Will chimed in. "Funnily enough, I reached out to Timantha to set me up on a date and, one look at her, I realized I didn't want anyone else," he said, turning to me and flashing that sinful smile.

Malika swooned. "Aww! So, Tim, you're a matchmaker?" She leaned in and lowered her voice. "It's okay if I call you Tim, right? I just love when girls have boy names."

I laughed. "It is fine, and yes, I am a matchmaker. It's still early days, but—" I coughed when Will grabbed my leg under the table, startling my thoughts away from me.

"She's being modest. She's a natural at what she does," he said, and I looked at him, confused.

We hadn't exchanged more than a few words since our encounter this morning. I sat in the hotel all day, trying to shake off the jetlag with a book in hand. Yet, every time Will came and left the suite to check on me, the tension between us was palpable, a thick fog that neither of us could pierce. I knew I had struck a nerve during breakfast, so I gave him space, using the day to rest and prepare for the week ahead.

Still, I couldn't shake the jarring feeling his reaction had left me with. Will was a walking contradiction. One moment, he draped me in fine jewelry, making me feel like a queen. The next, he had me pinned against a wall, terrified of his next move. His visceral inclination to push me away at the first sign of vulnerability cut deep, a raw reminder of the walls he kept firmly in place. A stark, painful reminder that this was definitely not the fairytale I had built up in my mind.

"And that ring!" Malika gushed, reaching across the table and grabbing my hand. "It's to die for!"

I pulled it back shyly. "Thank you. I told Will it was too much, but he didn't listen."

"I simply couldn't find a gem that rivaled her beauty," Will interjected, smiling, and I cut my eyes at him again. He almost looked like he meant it as he began stroking my thigh, signaling for me to calm down.

It bothered me that he was able to play this part so effortlessly. How he was able to pretend to be the doting husband when, moments before, he was cold and distant. But the way he was touching me, the way he put on a show for everyone around us, it was like I was observing a completely different man. Like once we stepped outside the doors of our suite, the charming Will Huntley reappeared, and all was right with the world again.

The duality of his personality was maddening, pulling me in with his magnetic charm only to push me away with his impenetrable walls. But if he thought he could simply turn me on and off like a light switch, he had another thing coming. I wasn't about to let him dictate my emotions so easily. Given that I was being paid to be here and didn't want to be stranded in the middle of Europe with no way home, I decided to give him the modified version of the Black woman's, *"fuck around and find out,"* treatment.

I would maintain my composure, play the role he expected, but I wouldn't let him trample over my feelings like I was some deal to be crushed. He needed to understand that my presence here wasn't just dictated by a paycheck. I demanded respect and appreciation for even playing along. If this was how he wanted to play, he'd soon realize that I wasn't one to back down easily. *Sorry, Will. This will hurt you more than it hurts me.*

Malika Conyers was more impressive in person than I could have even imagined. For dinner, she ordered for the entire table in French and then proceeded to tell us all the dessert selections without help from the waitstaff. The woman was *bad*—beautiful, elegant, and spoke three languages. She was everything I wanted to become, complete with a husband who looked at me the way Jeff looked at her.

"So where's the little one this evening?" Will asked, as we all devoured our desserts.

"We lucked out and ran into a business acquaintance who brought their nanny. So, J.R. was on a play date this evening," Malika's husband Jeff chimed in. So the man did speak.

"I heard you two were trying to get pregnant," Jeff continued just as I took a bite of my raspberry tarte. A rogue raspberry shot across the table, landing with a plop on Jeff's plate.

I coughed, my face flaming with embarrassment. "I am so sorry about that!"

Malika leaned forward with concern. "Oh honey, are you okay?"

Jeff and I both responded at the same time, "I'm fine," creating a moment of awkward synchronicity that made Will chuckle nervously.

Will handed me a handkerchief, his eyes twinkling with amusement. "Sorry to catch you off guard, honey. I hope you didn't mind that I shared that with Malika when I ran into her at that wedding I told you about?"

I took the handkerchief, my nails digging into Will's thigh under the table. "Again, I'm so sorry for my reaction. I just didn't realize we were telling people that we're trying ... *honey*," I said through gritted teeth, my eyes shooting daggers at him. Meanwhile, I cringed inwardly as I watched Jeff try to discreetly flick the raspberry off his plate, his attempt at subtlety only making the situation more awkward.

Pregnant? When was he going to clue me in on the fact that we were trying to get pregnant? I didn't know the first thing about trying, and now I was on the verge of a panic attack because I wasn't prepared. This lady seemed like the type to start asking me about ovulation kits and HCG levels. With any luck, I could simply agree and move this conversation along.

"It's just so daunting ... you know, the trying and the waiting. I try not to talk about it because I don't want the thoughts to consume me. I want to enjoy the making of the baby, and we've just heard so many stories about it becoming about simply getting pregnant and not enjoying the journey." I placed

123

my hand on Will's lap and felt him straighten in his seat. "And with this handsome man here, I don't want to miss out on enjoying *every part* of the baby-making journey, *if you know what I'm sayin'*," I said, moving my eyebrows up and down suggestively.

The table erupted in laughter.

"Well, it sounds like you've got the right attitude," Malika said with a wink. "Just enjoy the process, and let things happen naturally."

Jeff laughed, and it was the first time I'd seen him relax the entire evening. "Oh, yeah, and we know all about enjoying *that journey.*"

Will tried to put his hand on my thigh, but I swiftly took my nail and dug it into his hand, causing him to withdraw it quickly. He thought I was finally playing nice when I was getting ready to beat him at his own game. I kept my hand placed in his lap, gently moving it toward his groin area. I saw Will's expression turn concerned as he cut his eyes at me, trying to maintain a conversation. I pretended not to notice his gaze, laughing and feigning interest in what everyone else was saying.

"So, Tim, how did you get a guy like Will Huntley to settle down? The papers seem to have him pegged, but he seems different with you!" she observed, and I made a mental note to go and Google what was the big deal about this man. And why was he the most eligible bachelor I'd never heard of?

As an executive headhunter, I'd worked with men like Will for years. Most of them were all too eager to have people sing their praises and have buildings named after them. Will was arrogant and anal as all get out. But he wasn't boastful about his wealth, and even though I was still pissed at him, I found that to be refreshing.

I cleared my throat. "The better question is how did Will get *me* to settle down?"

Jeff made a face as if he was impressed, and Malika said, "A woman who knows her worth! I like her, Will!"

As Malika and Will began discussing the various activities planned for the week, including the big pitch fest on Saturday, my hand continued its exploration. The opulent tablecloths in the restaurant concealed my movements perfectly. No one could tell that my hand had just reached his impressive member, and that was when my fun began.

As payback for ... well ... everything, I decided to make the rest of the evening as uncomfortable as possible for Will. He grabbed my wrist, squeezing for me to stop, but I continued to stroke him beneath the table. He couldn't help but get harder and harder as Malika asked him about his firm's track record in the consumer packaged goods space. She was trying to get to know more about their business, but I didn't care and didn't let up. I stroked him as Will struggled for air and strength, fighting to maintain the conversation without revealing his arousal.

His jaw tightened, and his eyes flickered with a mix of frustration and fire. Every word he spoke was strained, his usual composure cracking under the pressure. I smiled sweetly, my hand relentless, reveling in the power shift. If Will thought he could control everything, he was about to learn that I wasn't one to be easily managed.

I was taking a sip of my wine with my left hand, my right otherwise occupied, when Malika asked, "So, Timantha,

125

any plans for you this week while you're here? I can't imagine you're okay sitting in the hotel room all day."

Will's hand slammed on the table, causing everyone's head to snap in his direction. "Baby, you look pale. Are you okay?" I asked, unrelenting in my torture.

"Mmmmhmmm," he growled, biting into his bottom lip so hard I saw blood.

"Yeah, bruh. You really don't look good," Jeff added, his eyebrows knitting in concern.

"I'm fine," Will said, taking a sip from his glass. "Tim, you were saying? About your plans this week?" he asked, trying to divert the attention away from himself.

"Oh! Right!" I jumped. "Well, this trip was sooo last minute for me that I hadn't actually had a chance to make plans. But, of course, I have to do some of the touristy things that everyone does in Paris," I said, gushing. Will began coughing and choking on his drink, his face turning a delightful shade of crimson.

Malika leaned in, her eyes sparkling with curiosity. "Oh, you must visit the Eiffel Tower and the Louvre! And don't forget the charming little cafes. They are to die for!"

Jeff, trying to be helpful, added, "But don't believe the hype when people tell you to try the escargot. It is *not* a must," he said, shivering.

Will, still struggling to maintain his composure, nodded vigorously. "Yes, yes, all of that ... escargot sounds ... fantastic," he managed to choke out, his voice strained.

I squeezed his thigh, my fingers still mischievously working their magic under the table. "Absolutely. I'm so looking forward to it," I said, giving Will a saccharine smile. His eyes widened, pleasure and panic flashing across his face. *He was close.*

"Baby, are you sure you don't need to excuse yourself?" I asked him, feigning concern, my tone dripping with faux innocence.

The man leveled me with the most murderous stare that I nearly peed my panties ... *or was that something else that was wet?* The intensity of his glare was enough to make me question my bravado for a split second.

"Timantha," Will managed to get out. "Remember you said you were *dying* to babysit for Malika and Jeff?" he asked, his voice smooth but laced with underlying mischief, causing me to pause my movements abruptly.

Will grinned, a triumphant look in his eyes. He knew I didn't like kids. "You know, they could really use a night out, and you did say you'd love to get some practice in with little J.R.," he added, leaning back in his chair with a smug expression.

We both looked at Malika and Jeff, who were grinning from ear to ear. "I mean, we thought Will was just saying that to get into my wife's good graces," Jeff said excitedly. "But if you're serious, we'd love to give you a firsthand experience of what it's like to have a baby."

I turned to Will, eyebrows raised. "What's this now?"

"Well, babe. I was telling Malika how you love babies and—"

127

"Get to the part about me babysitting," I demanded, cutting him off.

Will shifted in his seat, clearly enjoying the moment. "Malika mentioned that their nanny wouldn't be able to attend this week, and I sort of volunteered us to babysit for them if they needed."

I stared at him, my mouth slightly agape. "You sort of volunteered us?"

"Yeah, you know, since you're so great with kids and all," he said, trying to look innocent but failing miserably. *Oh, no ... he ... didn't.*

I let out the most nervous laugh, sounding like a drunken chimpanzee. "Umm, sweetie, I can't babysit. I don't have a CPR license. Don't babies require licensed practitioners or something?" I asked, dead serious, but everyone else found it amusing.

Jeff chuckled. "Don't worry, Timantha. You'll be fine. It's just for a few hours." *Okay seriously. This man was suddenly chatty Kathy when before he looked like he wanted to murder Will.*

I forced a smile, feeling the walls closing in. I did *not* like babies. I wasn't even sure if I wanted any. Every time the conversation came up among other women, I always felt defective because I didn't gush over the idea of having a big belly and swollen ankles. I enjoyed freedom, travel, and the ability to be kidnapped and whisked away to Paris on a moment's notice. I hated that I felt like I had to hide my true feelings on motherhood. Especially now that I was being thrown into something that would likely make me hate kids even more.

"I'll tell you what," Malika said as if she was dangling a carrot. "If you two babysit and let me and Jeff have a date night tomorrow, we'll bring you as our guests to the private party with DJ D-Nice on Thursday! What do you say?"

Will looked at me, confused, and I could tell he was about to ruin this. "Who's D—" Will was about to ask and I grabbed his penis under the table again to silence him.

I grew up on D-Nice, and I had been itching for an opportunity to go to one of his parties since he started Club Quarantine during the pandemic! He was not about to get in the way of making another one of my dreams come true!

"Deal! What time are we getting little Jeff Junior?" I asked.

"We call him J.R.," Jeff corrected, but I didn't care if they called that baby Chuckie. I was going to see D-Nice!

Chapter Eighteen

Will

I had no clue who D-Nice was, but somehow my brilliant scheme to get back at Timantha for her torturous antics backfired in the most unexpected way. Malika and her husband Jeff floated out of dinner on cloud nine after Timantha graciously agreed to babysit for them, dragging me into the deal. I don't know what on my face said that I could be trusted with a baby, but the plan might just win me some brownie points with Malika.

The elevator ride back up to our hotel room was fiery. On one hand, I was furious at the stunt Timantha had pulled at dinner. On the other hand, I wanted a repeat of the night before. She stood there opposite me in the elevator in a black cocktail dress, daring me to say something about the games she was playing.

"You think that was funny? What if Malika or her husband would have seen? What if you ruined this deal for me by making her think we were deviants or something?"

She threw her head back, laughing. "Deviant? Calm down, Dahmer. She probably would have respected you more for your wife not being able to get enough of you! Women love a man who is irresistible to his woman!"

I raised an eyebrow. "So, I'm irresistible to you?"

"You are a pain in my ass and a means to an end. What's irresistible is messing with you because you're so tightly wound that you think walking around with a hard on, instead of taking me the way you want, is the symbol of control."

"I'm not—" I muttered under my breath, but I stopped at the sight of her taking steps toward me.

She took her hand and placed it on my chest and traced a line with her hand down my stomach, stopping at my groin area. And, well ... *shit.*

"Just like I said," she whispered with a satisfied smile.

She backed away from me and leaned against the wall of the elevator car. "I've worked with men like you my entire career. I know the confident ones. The arrogant ones. The incompetent, privileged ones." I was staring down at the floor when she stopped talking, dipping her head so she could catch my gaze. "And I know the ones who have something inside them, stopping them from indulging in the good that they want. Either they feel they don't deserve it or can't handle it for some reason or another."

She didn't say she was talking about me, but she was definitely talking about me. And damn it, she was doing it again. She was seeing right through me, and I hadn't given her permission to be this close or get that deep.

I stood up straight, and my eyes darkened at the challenge in her eyes. "Come here," I commanded, my voice low and firm.

Her expression shifted to one of confusion, but she didn't move.

"Timantha, take three steps toward me, now," I said, this time my voice slightly more elevated so it echoed throughout the elevator car. And this time, she obeyed, stepping off of the wall and taking three steps toward me.

"Come closer," I said, lowering my voice to a growl. And she did as she was told.

I took her face in my hands and brought her mouth to mine. She was initially stunned, her hands outstretched and unsure of what to do. When I used my tongue to part her lips gently, she melted into me, moaning at the sensation of our tongues colliding.

Just as she was letting herself get carried away by the kiss, I broke our contact, and it took seconds for her to peel her eyelids open. "Why ... why'd you stop?" she breathed, and this time I grinned the satisfied grin.

"Next time, do as you're told the first time, and maybe you'll get more," I teased just as the elevator door opened to reveal our floor.

I wasn't sure if there would be a next time, but I needed a way to silence Timantha in that moment. "You did that on purpose!" she yelled behind me, and I grinned while greeting my security detail at our suite's entrance.

He opened the door for us before sliding me a report that detailed any suspicious activities or security briefings for the day. "You know what they say about payback, don't you?"

"That he's a rich asshole?"

The way things were headed between Timantha and me, I was on the brink of derailing this deal myself. If I didn't get a hold of my emotions and learn to be civil with her, I risked driving her away. I prided myself on being a professional who had closed hundreds of deals through my ability to stay focused and level-headed. Yet, with Timantha, I was failing miserably.

No matter how much I fought my desires for her internally, Timantha needed to feel like she was more than just a transaction to me. Achieving that would require me to let down my defenses a little, to show her a glimpse of the man behind the guarded persona.

She was getting ready to storm into her bedroom before I stopped her. "Timantha, wait," I said, my voice laced with remorse.

She turned around, and part of me wished she wouldn't have. The view from behind was *exquisite*. "What is it, Willow Huntley?"

I grinned. "Can we have a truce?"

"A truce requires the two of us to have been at war. You were a jerk to me, and I responded. That requires a different sort of agreement. One that begins with an apology and ends with *maybe* forgiving you."

"I'm sorry, Timantha. I'm beyond grateful for you being here this week, and I can do better. I can treat you better." I took a step closer to her. "I wish I could offer you more. I swear to God, for the first time in my life, I wish I could offer someone more. But this week is it."

I took a few more steps closer until I was just inches from her. "If I promise to be better, will you forgive me?"

She bit her bottom lip. "Under one condition," she said, and I shook my head at what was about to come next.

"What is it, Timantha?"

"I want more …"

"I already told you I can't give you anything more than this week."

"No, not that. I understand what this week is. I'm saying I want more of what you did in the elevator." *And there it was.*

"You're saying you want to be dominated, Timantha?" I watched as she walked into her bedroom, and I missed her already.

When she walked back in, she was holding the contract in her hand. "Read all the demands and changes I requested on page three," she said. "*That's* what I want, Willow Huntley." I was beginning to like the sound of my full name on her tongue.

When she'd told me before that she made those ridiculous changes, I didn't bother to check to see if she'd actually demanded those things. I didn't think she was serious. But as I flipped through the pages, the red ink in the margins suggested that she was absolutely serious. *And it would seem that the perfectly predictable Timantha was a freak.*

The next day, I arranged for Timantha to enjoy a spa appointment and a few tourist visits, accompanied by one of the men from my security detail. Meanwhile, I attended more meetings and presentations. Most of these summit meetings involved listening to men with inflated egos go on about their plans to revolutionize the technology landscape. Frankly, I was only interested in the few people I had intentionally set appointments with.

With our adventures in babysitting land beginning at six in the evening, I decided to make the most of our time beforehand. I ordered room service but asked the staff to elevate the experience to something special. Candlelight, elegant place settings, and a menu that rivaled any fine dining restaurant. To set the romantic mood, I even asked Timantha to get dressed up for dinner at four.

When she stepped out in a stunning, turquoise, strapless dress, her eyes sparkling with curiosity and surprise, I knew the effort had been worth it. The dress was simple, but she made it look like a fortune with the way the soft fabric flowed around her. A gold necklace adorned her neck, complementing the dress perfectly. Her elegance and beauty took my breath away, making the romantic setup feel like a scene from a fairy tale. Exactly as I'd planned.

I really was trying to be a better host for her. She didn't ask to be here, and I knew that by continuously pushing her away, I was actually making my chances at pulling this whole thing off worse. So, I made a conscious decision to make her feel like she was on an adventure and in one of her romance novels. I still wasn't sure if I was going to fulfill any of those requests in her contract amendments, though.

"Today was lovely. This dinner is amazing," she said, her smile radiant. "First the spa treatments earlier and this—candles, the food, the ambiance—you did good. You seem different."

"I told you I'd be better for you," I replied, my voice soft yet earnest.

"You still seem a bit guarded, though," she quipped, her tone playful but observant.

"Rome wasn't built in a day."

Taking a sip of her wine, she asked, "So, you ready to babysit tonight?"

I threw my head back in laughter. "Not at all! When I made the joke of you babysitting, I fully intended on being out for the night!" I confessed.

"You still could leave! It would serve me right after what I did to you!"

"Yeah, you're a cruel woman," I joked, knowing nothing was further from the truth.

"And while I'm not a fan of kids and avoid them like the plague, I won't leave you tonight. As much as you think you've done to torture me so far on this trip, I think we both know that I've done far worse. I appreciate you more than you know, Tim, and I wouldn't dare leave you to do this by yourself."

I was an entitled, selfish bastard at times. But it didn't mean I didn't have a heart. Timantha had a way of getting under my skin, but I'd come to enjoy the way we teased and pranked each other. It felt like she was opening up a part of me that I forgot existed.

She smiled, a hint of curiosity flickering in her eyes. "If this wasn't the arrangement that it was, do you think we would have ever ended up ..." She trailed off, shaking her head. "Never mind, it's a silly question."

I leaned in, captivated by the magical shade of brown her eyes took on under the candlelight. "Tell me. I'm sure it wasn't silly."

"I was going to ask if you thought there was ever a possibility where you and I could have ended up together. And it's silly because we're too different," she said, her voice tinged with uncertainty.

"Some people would say different—opposite—is a good thing," I said, my gaze unwavering.

"Some people are too idealistic for their own good," she quipped, a teasing smile playing on her lips.

"Do you want to know the answer?" I asked, leaning in slightly. She raised an eyebrow, intrigued.

"If you want to tell me," she said, taking another bite of her lamb.

"The truth is, I don't know," I admitted. "I've never been affected by a woman like you before. What I can tell you is that the story about my reaction when I first saw you—it was real."

She let out a sarcastic laugh. "Then why do you feel the need to torture yourself?" she asked, referring to my refusal to give in to my hunger for her that was quickly approaching starvation.

"I'm not torturing myself," I replied, shaking my head. "Let's just say I'm a smart businessman. The amount of pleasure you come with is not worth jeopardizing the amount of business on the line."

She paused, her fork hovering in mid-air, eyes locking onto mine. "So, what you're saying is ... I'm a risk?"

I nodded slowly. "A risk I can't afford to take lightly. But the truth is, the more time I spend with you, the harder it becomes to separate business from pleasure."

She softened, her sarcasm melting away. "Maybe some risks are worth taking."

I reached out, gently tucking a stray lock of hair behind her ear. "Maybe they are. But I need to figure out how to handle it without jeopardizing everything I've worked for. Without losing myself in something that could ruin me."

Her eyes searched mine, filled with understanding. "I get that," she said, holding my gaze.

As we sat there, the candlelight flickering softly between us, I realized that this moment—this fragile, beautiful connection—was worth any risk.

Chapter Nineteen

Timantha

Experiencing Will at dinner, relaxed and actually enjoying himself, reminded me of the glimpse of him I'd gotten on the plane. The glimpse that made me want to go on this little adventure with him. On the plane, he was quick witted, confident and sexy. Since we'd arrived in Paris, he'd been uptight and downright rude. Elevator escapades excluded.

At dinner, he seemed like he was into me. Like he might actually let his hair down and give in to his inhibitions. Handing him the contract was risky, but after that little display of dominance in the elevator, my panties were on fire and nowhere near being extinguished.

My phone started ringing, and I looked down to see that Tika was calling me from WhatsApp. "Girl! What are you doing awake? It's after midnight where you are!"

"I'm just checking in on you to make sure you haven't been unalived or anything!" she said, making me shake my head laughing.

"All is well, girl. This week has been crazy, and it's only Wednesday!"

Tika ignored my frivolous complaints about being whisked off in a private jet to Paris. "Yeah. Yeah. Cry me a river. How big is his dick?"

"Tika!"

"What!? We have book club tomorrow, and I was given explicit instructions to report back! Is it true what they say about white boys?"

"Tika!" I gasped.

"Oh girl. This is not the time to be private, prissy, and proper, okay?! You are living *all of our* wildest fantasies, and you must spill the details!"

I sighed, burying my face in my hands in mock shame. "I can't spill any details because there are no details to spill!" I confessed.

"Wait, what? Still? How is that possible? Is he paying you because he's using you as his beard or something?"

"No! He's not gay. I've confirmed at least that. He just has some sort of issue with letting himself fully let go. You know? Like he's afraid if he goes all the way there with me, that he will lose control or something."

"Ahh. He's got control issues. I bet he's got some really good kinks like S&M or something."

"That's what I said!" I fell onto my bed out of frustration. "I am in the most romantic city in the world, and I can't even get a romantic rendezvous?"

"Girl! I know you're the one who always makes sure we do things proper and ladylike." *If only she knew the things I'd been doing to try to get this man to break.* "But a man like that needs to own the situation from start to finish. So simple seduction doesn't do it for him," she observed, and I had to think about that for a moment because she was actually right.

Men like Will Huntley were propositioned and come on to all the time, and it's why he had such control when it came to my girlish advances. But I hadn't tried the forbidden fruit route. The route where I make him hurt so badly for me that he's begging.

"Remember that one dark romance we read," Tika continued. "The one by Milly Trois where the female lead played so unbelievably hard to get that the man was ready to propose marriage by the time she was done with him?"

I gasped. "Yes! I remember that one! Oohh that's a great idea, T!"

Milly Trois, obviously a pen name, was one of our favorite dark romance authors. Every time she dropped a new book, we flocked to her website to purchase her special edition copies and any goodies that came with them. She was known for writing stories about badass women—irresistible forces to be reckoned with. And it suddenly hit me that I was playing this game all wrong when it came to Will. Throwing myself at him was child's play. I needed to become someone irresistible.

I hung up with Tika when I heard a knock on the door of our suite. It was just before six in the evening, so I assumed it was Malika and her husband coming to drop off the baby. Will was an ass for volunteering me for this, but I decided to face it head-on.

Before I went back into the living room to greet Malika, I decided to change into something a little more comfortable. Instead of the baggy sweats I had planned on wearing, I put on matching blue yoga pants and a sports bra. I swept my kinky curls into a bun, allowing a few messy curls to hang loose sporadically. I wasn't going for overly seductive; I was aiming for a relaxed, sexy vibe that appeared like I didn't care about how I looked.

As I emerged from the bedroom, Will's eyes widened slightly at the sight of me. Malika and her husband were at the door, cradling little J.R. in their arms. I greeted them with a warm smile, feeling a newfound confidence in my casual yet alluring appearance. Tonight was going to be a test, and I fully planned on Will failing miserably.

"Thank you both again for agreeing to babysit for us!" Malika said, grinning.

"It's really no trouble at all," Will said, and I snickered at his faked enthusiasm. He was no more prepared for this than I was, and I forgot to coordinate who would be on diaper duty because it was certainly not going to be me.

Malika and Jeff left us with instructions, baby food, a few changes of clothes, and extra bottles, and Will and I both looked like we were getting ready to walk the Green Mile. We sat the baby down in the travel play pin, and he just looked at us both.

"What do we do with it?" Will asked.

I shrugged. "It seems fine now, so I feel like we take the 'if it ain't broke, don't fix it' route right now."

Will looked at me, astonished. "I thought you said you had siblings."

"I do, but by the time I met them, they had hair and could wipe their own ass, so excuse me for being clueless right now!"

142

"Okay, why don't you keep it company, and I will go put the bottles and food in the fridge?"

"Why do I have to watch it? You're the one trying to get into its mommy's favor! You watch it!"

"I think we probably should stop referring to it as ... it," Will suggested.

"Ahh, you're right." I looked at the little, chubby cheeks and then back at Will. "What was his name again?"

"Timantha!" He gasped.

"What!? I don't know this little boy! How am I supposed to remember it's—*his*—name!?"

Ultimately, things started off relatively smoothly. We played peek-a-boo, fed him some mashed peas, and even managed to get him to laugh with a few ridiculous faces. Will was starting to relax, his cool demeanor returning as he and I took turns cooing at J.R., who seemed to adore me, by the way.

Will was putting the baby's food away when he started to cry. "Is that you or the baby crying?" Will asked from the kitchen.

"It's the both of us!" I yelled with a fake whine, and when Will came back over to us, we both just stood there and looked at the baby screaming.

"You know, I once saw on TikTok where a dad didn't know what to do when his baby was crying, so he started crying and yelling back in his baby's face and the baby stopped."

Will's head slowly turned toward me as if I'd just said to go play with the baby in traffic. "Are you seriously suggesting that we yell in the baby's face?"

"I don't know what I'm saying! Why did you volunteer me for this!?"

"Because your hand was vigorously rubbing my junk under the dinner table, and it was the only way to get you to stop!" he muttered through gritted teeth. Meanwhile, the baby was still screaming at the top of his lungs.

Then it happened.

The sound was unmistakable. A rumbling, gurgling noise that could only mean one thing. My eyes widened in horror. "Will … is that what I think it is?"

"Okay, let's not panic," he said, not sounding the least bit convincing. "I remember from a movie I saw once where they smelled the diaper. Maybe he needs a diaper change," Will said, and I immediately stepped away from the play pen.

"Yeah, diapers are where I draw the line so … ummm, good luck with that!"

I watched Will inch close to the baby's diaper like he was trying to avoid setting off a bomb. "Oh … oh my God. That … that smells disgusting," Will said, plugging his nose and looking like he was threatening to vomit.

"What is it?"

"It's shit, Timantha," he said sarcastically, making me burst into laughter. "Would you please help me? I don't think I can do this on my own." Witnessing him beg was sort of cute.

I let out a sigh. "Okay, fine. Where do you want me?"

"Can you get his changing mat out of his diaper bag and lay it on the floor? Then I'll pick up the baby and put him on it."

I could handle that, so I went to the diaper bag and proceeded to look for the changing mat. "Umm, Will? Which one is the changing mat?" There were too many things that could be used to simply lay a baby on.

"It will have plastic on one side. You know, so it's easy to clean off if a mess is made?"

I bunched my eyebrows together. "How would you know that? I thought you didn't know anything about babies?" He didn't answer, but it struck me as odd that he would know such an odd detail.

I found the changing pad and brought it over to Will and placed it on the ground next to him. Will gently grabbed the baby, who was still screaming, and placed him down on the mat like he was a fragile piece of glass. He never said hadn't been around kids, but I'd just assumed that someone of his caliber wouldn't have any insight. But he seemed like he'd done this before.

When he got the baby's pants off and opened the diaper, the contents made me call on Jesus. It was bad. Really bad. The kind of bad that made you question how something so small could produce something so ... vast. Will's face twisted in a mixture of disgust and determination as he removed the diaper and folded it into a tight ball. *How was he so good at this?!*

He placed the soiled diaper in a plastic bag and then proceeded to pick up the baby and carry him to the kitchen. "Where are you going with it?" I asked, and Will just laughed.

145

"Come on, we're gonna wash him up in the sink. Grab the diaper bag and find him a change of clothes, and I'll wash him up."

I swooned and suddenly remembered I was supposed to be playing hard to get. But watching this man handle this baby with care had me reverting back to the feral woman I was acting like the night before.

Will gave J.R. a bath in the sink, and I listened as he talked to him. No baby talk or cooing or anything like that. But he held a conversation with him like he was another person.

I leaned against the kitchen counter. "You talk to him like he understands what you're saying," I said, smiling, and both of the boys looked in my direction as if to say J.R. knew exactly what I was saying.

"Babies understand more than you think," Will said.

"How *do* you know so much about babies? Because just when I think I've got you pegged, you throw me for another loop, Willow Huntley."

He smirked, then gave me the most tortured stare. I could tell he was deciding whether or not to share a piece of his truth. "I had a daughter," he said softly before returning his attention back to J.R.

The baby was playing with a plastic spoon in the water, and Will kept his eyes on the baby. "Had?" I probed.

"She didn't pass away or anything, if that's what you're thinking." He smiled, but it didn't fully meet his eyes. It wasn't the kind of smile you donned when you were happy. It was the one you smile when things are ironic.

146

"When Miranda, my fiancé, told me she was pregnant, I have to admit I was overjoyed," he said, taking a cup of water and rinsing J.R.'s back. "Even though I couldn't make it to all her appointments and birthing classes, she said she understood that I was working to provide for them."

Will finally looked up at me, but he didn't say what I thought he would. He simply asked, "Would you mind bringing me a towel so we can dry him off?"

I quietly retreated to my bathroom and came back with a clean towel. "Thank you," he said, and I just stood there silently, willing him to continue his story.

"When Chloe—we named her after my sister—was six months old, she developed a blood infection that required a blood transfusion. But because of her rare blood type, she could only have blood donated from a relative. Her type limited her to only having a parent donate."

"Oh no," I said, guessing what he was about to say next.

"Exactly. Neither of us were a match. Chloe had a rare blood type that could only be mixed with the same type. Even though Miranda was a DNA match and we confirmed she was Chloe's mother, the only way Chloe could have a different blood type from both of us was if I wasn't her father."

"Willow, I'm so sorry," I whispered, and for the first time since continuing his story, he met my gaze.

"You insist on calling me Willow."

"I insist on knowing the real you."

He took the towel from my hands and wrapped J.R. in it so snugly. I marveled at the gentle way he rubbed lotion on him and got him ready for bed.

It was a rare and touching moment to have Will open up to me. He was usually so guarded, so distant, that no one would ever suspect he had been through something so deeply human. Despite all my research, I never came across any mention of a fiancée named Miranda. He must have gone to great lengths, and spent a fortune, to erase her from his life after such a heartbreaking betrayal. He didn't talk about her any more after that, though. He was closed back off just as quickly as he'd opened up.

"I think I left his pajamas on my bed when I was looking for his food earlier. Watch him for me while I go grab them?" Will jumped up, leaving the baby swaddled on the floor before I could protest.

J.R. started crying, and watching Will handle him so effortlessly made me feel like I could do it too. How hard could it be? I walked over to him and picked him up. Remembering that I always saw people bounce a crying baby, I stood up and began bouncing while simultaneously singing.

"Baby shark! Doo doo! Doo doo doo!" And he actually started laughing. Never having seen a baby laugh up close before, I pulled him back away from my shoulder and smiled at the chubby cheeks laughing at me.

"Will! It ... he's laughing! I'm getting the hang of this!"

"Good job!" Will praised from the other room.

I started singing the Baby Shark song some more, hoping to get more laughs, and sure enough, the baby laughed! I was a hit! Maybe this baby thing wasn't so hard after all. I wouldn't commit to birthing one, but babysitting might not be off the table any longer!

I was bouncing and singing to J.R. with the words I made up to Baby Shark, when I suddenly felt a constant stream of warmth running down my breasts. I looked down, and I screamed the biggest shriek as it hit me. "You didn't put another diaper on him!" The little shit was peeing on my boobs!

My screams must have startled the baby because he immediately started crying. "Will! Help!" I cried, but it was too late. J.R. let out an ugly burp, followed by a stream of baby vomit that landed squarely on my face. I'm not proud of what happened next.

I don't know how it happened or what told my brain to do this but … I threw the baby. Like thrust him into the air far away from my face as vomit streamed out of that baby's mouth. Thankfully, Will caught him.

"Did you just throw the baby?"

"I handed him to you!"

"You threw the baby."

"No! I enthusiastically put him in your arms!"

"Yeah! Through the air!"

I had to hand it to him, though. Will caught J.R. with a miraculous dive, cradling him against his chest like he was a football. "Hey there, buddy," he said softly, trying to calm him down.

"Will you do me a favor and heat up his bottle? Heat it up for thirty seconds and then shake it. And heat it up for thirty seconds more," he instructed, and I'd swear my uterus contracted at the sound of it.

He put the baby into his pajamas, gave him his bottle, and then rocked him to sleep.

"I'm going to go shower while it's calm," I said, pointing to the vomit- slash urine-soaked mess that was my outfit.

Will laughed. "Put your clothes in one of the laundry bags, and I'll make sure it's cleaned. Shame though," he said in a low voice. "You looked good in that."

I winked. "Wait until you see what I look like with it off," I said before walking into my room and closing the door.

Chapter Twenty

Will

Malika and Jeff arrived to pick up J.R. while Timantha was in the shower, and I had them doubled over with laughter as I recounted how the baby had peed and thrown up all over her. Of course, I conveniently omitted the part about Timantha launching their baby into the air like a football. All in all, they were thoroughly impressed, and Malika finally accepted my meeting invite for Friday. It seemed that building a friendship with her was starting to pay off.

When Timantha emerged from her room, dressed in a matching silk pajama short set, I found myself wishing we could rewind time, placing the baby back between us. Sharing that part of my story with her wasn't planned. I hadn't spoken about Miranda and Chloe since it all happened, and everyone else in my circle knew not to bring her up. Once I stopped talking about the incident, I made sure it was wiped from my senses. But with Timantha, maybe I wanted her to know me. Perhaps a part of me needed her to understand why I had to keep her at a distance.

I'd met Miranda at a charity gala, one of those glittering events where everyone mingles under chandeliers and the air hums with the promise of power deals. She was the daughter of real estate royalty, effortlessly elegant and poised. From the moment I saw her, I knew she wasn't right for me. But she fit into my world better than most. Her father was a powerhouse in the industry, much like me, and she seemed to understand the demands of my life. So, I stayed with her, convincing myself that her seamless integration into my social and professional circles made up for the nagging feeling that something was off.

Our relationship carried on, marked by my long hours at work and her impeccably planned social calendar. I assumed she didn't mind my absence—after all, her father had been the same way, and she grew up in that environment. But I was wrong. I'm not blaming myself for her actions; she made her choices. Yet, the moment she looked me in the eyes and told me she'd cheated because she missed me, I felt a pang of guilt. Part of me knew I had played a role in the demise of our relationship, even if I wasn't the one who ultimately shattered it.

"Thank you for cleaning everything up. You didn't have to do it all by yourself," Timantha said, pulling me from my thoughts. She moved to pour herself a glass of wine, the liquid catching the light as it swirled in her glass.

"It was the least I could do. I figured you had your hands full cleaning the vomit out of your hair."

"Yeah, thanks for that." She laughed, the sound light and infectious. She moved gracefully to sit next to me on the couch, the scent of her lavender body wash lingering in the air.

As she turned toward me, I couldn't help but notice her piercings peeking through the thin fabric of her pajama top, betraying her lack of a bra. Her eyes were intense, her voice softer now. "Do you still talk to Chloe, or did you make a clean break?"

I let out a heavy sigh, unprepared for this line of questioning. "I figured she was young enough for me to make a clean break without it impacting her."

"What about you?" she asked, her voice barely above a whisper, her hand reaching out to cover mine. "Did it impact you?"

"Every day," I confessed, the words slipping out before I could stop them. She squeezed my hand, and in that moment, the need for distance dissolved into nothingness. My desire for her, always lurking beneath the surface, surged forward, impossible to deny. I pulled her on top of me, my hands roaming over the silk of her pajamas, the fabric a poor barrier against the heat of her skin. Every touch, every breath, was laced with a tortured desire, a longing that had been kept at bay for too long.

Her body fit against mine as if she were made for me, her breath coming in shallow gasps that mirrored my own ragged need. The silk of her pajamas whispered against my skin, amplifying the tension between us. My hands moved with a mind of their own, mapping out the planes of her body, committing every inch to memory.

I dipped my head to kiss her, but she didn't let me. "Don't do this again," she warned, her breath hitching as she pulled back just before our lips met. "Don't start something you won't be able to finish for whatever tortured reason you tell yourself tonight."

I wrapped my arm around her waist and stood, ignoring her protest. When I placed her gently on her feet, she looked up at me, her petite frame only reaching my chest, her eyes wide with anticipation and defiance. "What did I tell you, Timmy? I have to dictate what happens between us. Do you understand?"

She nodded, but I needed more.

"I didn't hear you."

"Yes," she whispered, the word trembling on her lips.

"Good. Sweet girl," I murmured, a slow smile spreading across my face. "Now, go into your room and bring me that smutty book you've had your nose in."

She hesitated for a moment, then turned and walked away, the sway of her hips accentuated by the soft silk clinging to her body. The air was thick with a palpable tension, an unspoken promise of what was to come.

Chapter Twenty-One

Timantha

I didn't know what had transpired between yesterday and this evening, but Will had transformed in ways that left me breathless. The guarded, rigid demeanor he once wore like armor had melted away, revealing a man of controlled intensity and commanding presence. The change was magnetic, downright sexy.

Not sure what he wanted with it, I ran to my room and grabbed the latest Milly Trois dark romance novel, *Sinful Secrets of a Billionaire*. It was a dark, marriage of convenience romance about a tortured CEO who refused to allow himself to fall in love because he carried around guilt for his first wife dying in childbirth, which he wasn't present for.

When I'd gotten back into the living room, my book in hand, Will had removed the hoodie from the jogging suit he was wearing so he only had on a tank top and jogging pants. Gray ones. Seeing him dressed down was almost as sexy as seeing him dressed up, and I wondered if there was anything he didn't look good in. He sat on the couch, sipping a brown drink, patiently waiting for me to return. The man was built like an MMA fighter, and my body was begging to be annihilated.

"Sit there," he commanded, pointing to the chair opposite the sofa, his tone leaving no room for argument.

"You don't want me to sit next to you?" I questioned, but he simply stared straight ahead, ignoring my plea.

155

This man's ability to switch his moods and control his intensity at will was nothing short of astonishing. Each glimpse I caught of him revealed a new facet, making him seem like a different person every time. This dominant version of him felt familiar yet distinct, an intriguing blend I had never fully experienced before. All I knew was that I craved whatever he was willing to give. This was the most invigorating encounter of my life, and we were only just getting started.

Reluctantly but enthusiastically, I crossed the room to the burgundy wingback chair, settling in with my book. His eyes followed my every move, and it didn't matter how clothed I was, I suddenly felt naked.

"Is that the smut you talk about?" he asked, his voice low and tantalizing.

A flush crept up my neck. "It is," I admitted, my voice barely above a whisper.

"Does it have the love scenes you enjoy?" His eyes darkened with an intensity that made my pulse race.

I nodded, feeling the heat rise in my cheeks. "It does."

"Read one to me," he demanded, his tone brooking no refusal. My breath hitched at his request, my heart pounding wildly in my chest.

This was a side of him I'd been waiting for—dominant, commanding, and incredibly sexy. It didn't mean I wasn't nervous to comply. "Ex … excuse me?" I stammered, my voice barely above a whisper.

Will grinned but remained silent, a clear display of the power he wielded. It was my job to obey, no questions asked.

156

I turned to chapter fifteen of the book, my fingers trembling as I stared at the pages. The reality of what I was about to do was overwhelming, yet it was everything I had ever fantasized about when it came to these books.

"So, in this scene," I began to explain, but Will shook his head, his expression filled with displeasure.

"What?"

"I don't want you to summarize, Timantha. I want you to read me the words that make your mouth dry and your panties wet," he ordered, his voice a dark caress as his words sent a shiver down my spine. Immediately, I felt my body respond exactly as he described. *Mouth dry. Panties wet.*

Swallowing hard, I began to read, my voice trembling but steadying as the words flowed from my lips, the tension between us thickening with every syllable.

"Savannah was tired of feeling ignored by Marco. She knew she'd signed up for a marriage of convenience, but she never signed up for a marriage without passion."

I paused, glancing up to see Will's reaction. His eyes locked onto mine, dark and intense, threatening to set me ablaze with his gaze alone.

"I didn't tell you to stop," he said, his voice low and commanding.

"Sorry," I whispered, feeling the heat rise in my cheeks.

"Don't apologize. Continue."

I swallowed and resumed reading. "She marched into Marco's office where he'd been spending most nights. He hadn't touched her since their wedding night, nearly three months ago. The usual tricks of changing her hair and wardrobe weren't working, so she decided she was going to take matters, and her orgasms, into her own hands.

"It was clear that Marco was on a call. His tie was disheveled, and he was bent over his desk, yelling into the speakerphone. He put the call on mute to inform her that he was in the middle of a conversation with Tokyo, but she ignored him, even when he shouted for her to leave.

"There were two leather cigar chairs opposite Marco's desk, and Savannah took the liberty of sitting in one. She spread her legs, revealing she wore nothing beneath her red, silk lingerie. Marco's demands grew more insistent, demanding to know what she was doing or for her to leave, but Savannah remained silent, her eyes fixed on him with a challenging gleam."

As I read, my voice grew huskier, matching the escalating tension in the scene. Will's gaze never wavered, his intensity searing into me, making it clear he expected nothing less than my full compliance. The room crackled with unspoken desire, each word drawing us deeper into the tantalizing game.

"Instead, Savannah stuck her middle finger in her mouth, sucking it and circling her tongue around it until it was nice and damp, before she took it and began playing with her clit."

"Shit," I heard Will whisper, and my eyes shot up to meet his. We stared at each other for a few long, charged seconds before he broke the silence.

"Show me," he commanded.

By then, I knew better than to ask questions. With a trembling breath, I took my middle finger and put it in my mouth, mimicking the movements described in the book. My tongue swirled around it, wetting it thoroughly, the act both a submission and a statement. Will's eyes darkened with a raw, primal hunger, his gaze never leaving mine.

I started to slip my hand into my silk shorts when he held up a hand in protest. "According to your book, I should be able to see that you aren't wearing any panties."

I stood from the chair. But before I went any further, I needed to be sure. I couldn't let him wind me up only to leave me hot and bothered for the rest of the night. "Will, I swear if you're playing some game with my emotions and libido right now …"

He stood abruptly, silencing my thoughts in mid-air. His hands cupped my face, and he kissed me furiously, a raw, hungry passion driving his every move. I wrapped my arms around his waist, pulling him closer, but he suddenly backed away, breaking our connection.

In one swift motion, he bent down, yanking my pajama shorts down so fast I barely had time to react. As I steadied myself on his back and stepped out of the shorts, he remained crouched, his eyes locked onto mine. My nakedness was on full display, my clit mere inches from his mouth, yet his gaze never wavered.

"You're stunning," he breathed, his voice filled with reverence and desire. Without another word or warning, he sucked my clit into his mouth, and I doubled over with pleasure, gripping his shoulders for support. The intensity of the sensation was overwhelming, sending waves of ecstasy coursing through my body.

"Fuuuuck! Will!" I yelped, and he stopped just as quickly as he began. "See what I mean?" I yelled. "Torture!"

Will smiled as he backed away and took his place back on the sofa. "Sit down and show me how you play with your pussy, sweet girl, and don't you dare come until I give you permission." And fuck if I didn't come apart at his words alone.

He watched as I pleasured myself, his eyes lighting up with excitement while darkening with desire.

"Keep reading," he commanded, his voice a seductive growl. With my book in my left hand and my right hand exploring my body, I continued.

"That's it, sweet girl," he praised, his words sending waves of pleasure rippling through me. I saw him begin to unbutton his pants, his movements deliberate and slow.

"Savannah's husband tried to continue his call, but his attempt was unsuccessful when he watched as Savannah plunged three fingers inside herself."

I saw Will squeeze his throbbing hardness through the fabric of his joggers. "Show me," Will growled, his voice dripping with raw need.

I did as I was told, my fingers moving in rhythm with the words I read, the air between us thick with tension and unspoken promises. As the scene unfolded, the room seemed to close in around us, our shared desire becoming the only reality. The boundaries between fiction and reality blurred, and in that moment, nothing else mattered but the intense connection we were forging.

Will reached for his hardened length, and I could tell it was throbbing to break free. My rhythm paused as he unzipped his pants, and I licked my lips with anticipation.

"I didn't tell you to stop," he said, and so I continued with my exploration.

"Savannah's husband ended his call but didn't approach her. He just watched as she moaned and screamed while she chased her peak. She lifted her silk gown up farther, revealing her breasts as she played with her nipples, her hand still wreaking havoc on her center."

By then, Will's dick was on full display, and my eyes went wide at the sight of it. *The girls from the book club would be pleased.*

"Show me, Timantha. Let me see those beautiful breasts, sweet girl," he growled, and I continued playing along, reenacting everything Savannah was doing in the book.

I set the book down, lifting my silk blouse to reveal my hardened nipples with both piercings, and I rolled them between the fingers of my left hand. When I looked up, Will was stroking himself at the sight of me. I gulped as I saw drips of condensation leak from the tip.

My body was overheating as I was seconds from erupting. "Don't you come until I tell you to," Will demanded, and my eyes shot open at his words.

I understood the power and domination thing, but this was taking it a step far. How was I supposed to control my orgasm when I was watching his hand greedily stroking his length. If he was going to make me wait to come, then I was going to make him come quicker.

I took my silk blouse all the way off and wet my thumb and middle finger before massaging my nipples with my left and while continuing to allow my orgasm to build.

I kept my eyes on Will while pressure built in my core. "Is this what you like, Mr. Huntley?"

"Fuck, Tim. Don't say my name ... don't look at me like that, Tim. You're gonna make me ..." he growled.

"I'm going to make you what? I'm sorry your words drifted off a bit there," I teased as I threw my leg across the arm of the chair, giving him an even better view.

"So fucking beautiful. That's it, sweet girl," he muttered before he exploded on his stomach without any warning. "Shit! Fuck!"

As I watched his body tremble with pleasure, my eruption was seconds behind him. "Can I come, Mr. Huntley? Please can I come?"

Will nodded yes as my hands massaged my wet, slick folds. With his silent permission, I grabbed my breasts, arching my back as my orgasm crashed into me. Will watched with a sexy grin, his eyes dark with satisfaction as random curse words flew from my mouth.

Afterward, we cleaned ourselves up, the air still thick with the afterglow of our shared passion. Will led me to the shower, his touch gentle but possessive as he worshiped my body from head to toe. First with his hands, then with his mouth, and then his tongue.

As the warm water cascaded over us in the shower, I smiled, realizing that he had given me the first amended request that I'd made in our contract.

Chapter Twenty-Two

Will

The way the evening ended with Timantha was far from what I had imagined when I promised to be better for her. I couldn't understand what had come over me, but the moment I allowed her access to my memories of Chloe and revealed the pain I carried, it felt like nothing was off limits. I wanted to give her everything. I wanted to give her me.

I still hadn't shown her the full extent of my proclivities when it came to how I liked to *play*. But there were layers and levels to that life, and I didn't enter into any situation that involved domination lightly. We would need time. We would need trust. And I would need full control, her complete cooperation.

I was a greedy man, so I'd had my fill of women of all kinds. But never had a woman been able to satisfy me so completely while simultaneously leaving me aching for more. It wasn't just her body that fascinated me. I loved the way she thought, how she challenged me, and how she was inspiring me to try things and be someone I'd never even considered before meeting her. She was everything I imagined she'd be from the first moment I laid eyes on her, and I was already dreading letting her go.

I'd never understood women's fascination with romance novels until last night. When I was a kid, you couldn't tell me that Hustler and Playboy magazines weren't all about romance. The way the women were smiling and the joy it brought the hearts of young men across America, there had to be stories about love in them. But once Timantha started reading her book to me, I realized what women enjoyed was something entirely different than men. And it was addicting.

Women had been reduced to objects or tools that didn't have desires of their own, often painted as enemies to the desires of men. It was why there was such a barbaric attitude towards *taking* and owning. But after reading what Timantha enjoyed in her romance novels, I realized that women actually enjoyed being dominated by a man so long as they felt cherished. They didn't mind being taken and owned, so long as they understood the power they wielded over their men as well. And while Timantha was in the shower getting ready for the day, I found myself peeking into her novel, hoping to catch another glimpse of what she enjoyed. How I could please her later.

Just as I had predicted, one taste of Timantha had me abandoning my responsibilities. As if on cue, I woke up this morning, canceled meetings with people I had no interest in meeting with, and scheduled a private tour of the Louvre with Timantha instead. It was another one of the amendments she'd made in our contract—she wanted to be treated like royalty and be given a private tour of the famous museum. With the types of people and money I had at my disposal, it was one of the easier requests to fulfill. We would have to skip the "sex in a dark corner" part, though.

"I'm ready," Timantha sang, and I looked up to find her wearing the most adorably chic ensemble. A pink and black tweed blazer over a white blouse with a black bowtie, and black leather shorts that showed off her glorious legs. She completed the look with a black, leather painter's hat.

165

"You look beautiful," I said, unable to hide the way she made my heart skip several beats.

"Thank you," she replied, coming over to adjust my tie.

Or so I thought. Instead, she began untying it and taking it off. "Not a fan of the tie?"

She scrunched her nose adorably. "Not for a day of being a tourist. You look like you're going to a business meeting."

"It's a black suit with a baby blue shirt. I look like an Italian gigolo," I joked.

She laughed, the sound like music to my ears. "Well, without the tie, you look suave," she said, smiling, and I shrugged, letting her win that battle. If she said I looked suave, I was inclined to believe her.

I normally had a very regimented way I liked to dress. I had this suit brought by as a way to try something different, something that would complement her. Match her fly, as the kids liked to say.

"Well, if you're done grooming me, Mom, we need to get going. I've got reservations at the Louvre in two hours, and I wanted to take you to breakfast somewhere special before our tour."

Her eyes lit up with excitement. "Somewhere special?"

I smiled, remaining silent as I led her out the door to the surprise that awaited her—a private picnic on a boat as we sailed along the Seine River.

Her eyes widened in delight when she saw the setup. "Oh my goodness, Will! This is incredible!"

"I wanted to do something memorable," I said softly, guiding her onto the boat.

"Mission accomplished!" she said, beaming.

As we sailed down the Seine, the early morning light casting a golden glow over the city, I couldn't help but feel like this was a turning point for us. Timantha's laughter echoed across the water, blending with the gentle lapping of the waves against the boat. We sat down to a beautifully laid-out picnic, complete with croissants, fresh fruit, and champagne.

"To a perfect day in Paris," I toasted, raising my glass.

"To a perfect day," she echoed, her eyes meeting mine with a warmth that made my heart race. "And thank you for making yet another thing on my list in the contract a reality."

We clinked glasses and settled into the moment, the city of love providing the perfect backdrop for what felt like the beginning of something truly special. Something like love.

Chapter Twenty-Three

Timantha

The day started with a dreamy boat ride, drifting through the morning mist, followed by a tour of the Louvre that left me breathless. I didn't know what to expect from this trip, or from Will, but as the week drew to a close, I realized everything had far surpassed my wildest dreams. And to think, I was being paid to experience all of this.

I tried to push the thought of payment to the back of my mind—especially now that Will and I had crossed the line of intimacy. But the way he cherished me afterward, treating me with a tenderness that felt almost regal, made it impossible for those negative thoughts to linger. I refused to let the idea of this being anything less than magical ruin the incredible time I was having with him.

Thursday night had arrived, and with it, the much-anticipated party with Malika and her husband, featuring DJ D-Nice! Not knowing what Will had packed for the trip, I decided to take matters into my own hands. I enlisted his security team to grab a few stylish pieces that would be perfect for the evening. So far, all I had seen were stuffy suits, and those simply wouldn't do for a night with D-Nice.

"I haven't worn pants with stripes or designs on them since I was ten years old," Will muttered as I stood back and observed the outfit I'd picked out for him.

"The correct name for these are Chinos."

He let out a huff. "I don't care what they're called, they are tight at the ankles, and I won't be able to wear my loafers with these."

I laughed. "Oh, honey! You don't wear loafers with these!" I teased. "I used some of my per diem to have these white Air Force 1's with the black swoosh delivered for you."

He stared at me with a straight face. "Is this a costume party?"

"Oh my goodness! Would you just trust me? I know for a fact that you were about to put on one of your sad suits tonight, and no husband of mine is going to leave the house like that. This outfit makes you look stylish and like you belong to me," I said, glancing up at him once the words I'd said registered.

"I like the sound of that," he said, sending a puddle instantly to my panties.

His security guard knocked on the door, signaling our car had arrived to take us to the exclusive event.

On the drive there, Will uncharacteristically held my hand. "Are you nervous?" I asked, staring down at the way our skin blended together like milk and honey.

"A little. But not for the normal reasons."

"Your pants look fine," I said under my breath.

He smirked. "Not that. I'm usually nervous to say the wrong thing when it comes to business. Tonight, I'm nervous to say the wrong thing when it comes to you. This feels more like your domain, and I don't want to embarrass you."

His admission was unexpected, but it made my face hot. This man was rich, sexy, and successful, yet he was nervous about embarrassing me? I felt the urge to pinch myself but decided against it.

"You'll do fine," I reassured him, then shifted the conversation to help him relax—business. "How have your meetings been this week? I know you haven't met with Malika and her team yet, but you had other prospects as well, right?"

"Yes, and they've all gone very well. The problem is that those companies aren't going to be the brands that take our business into the future. So our investments will be minimal. We need a bigger win—a win like Malika's."

"I see. Well, tonight will be just as important as any," I assured him.

He shifted in his seat, and the way those pants fit him, combined with the way his white polo hugged his arms, had me ready to request we turn the car around. "What makes this evening so important? I thought you just wanted to see this DJ."

"It's not *just* about the DJ," I explained. "I want to see the DJ, sure. But seeing us in this type of environment will show Malika that you have a fun side outside of work."

He sat back in his seat, never letting go of my hand. "I guess you're right." He let out a sigh before taking my wrist and bringing it to his mouth. "We're a team, right? Tonight, we're a team?"

He seemed more nervous than he let on. The crowds of unfamiliar people, the potential business deal at stake, the fake wife on his arm—it was enough to make anyone anxious. For someone who already suffered from extreme anxiety, it was a recipe for disaster.

I leaned over to Will and brought his mouth to mine. "You got this, and I've got you," I said as I pulled away from our connection.

Will seemed to relax instantly after that, but the kiss only made him hungry for more. He leaned back over, placing a gentle hand on my neck as he dove deeper into my mouth, his tongue licking and sucking my bottom lip.

I pulled back, dangerously close to straddling this man. "You're going to ruin my lipstick," I said, panting.

"Good," he replied, also breathless. But I shifted to the other side of the seat to put some space between us.

His gaze followed me, and I'd never get used to the heat that immediately flowed between us whenever I caught him staring at me. I was wearing a white pencil skirt and matching white lace bralette. A few seconds more, and that skirt might have ended up over my head.

When we arrived at the location, it looked like an abandoned building. Will and I waited in the car while the driver went to the door and let the bouncer know who had arrived. We watched as the big, muscular man spoke into an earpiece before signaling it was okay to enter. Once we entered the building, it was like we were transported into one of the speakeasies of the Harlem Renaissance. The club was unmistakably Parisian, but the vibe was one hundred percent rhythm with a side of blues.

As we ventured deeper into the club, various shades of brown and gold glimmered in the evening lights. People smiled and greeted us as we walked by, many people smiling at the sight of me and Will.

Will leaned in to whisper something in my ear, his hand on the small of my back. "So, do Black people always magically find opportunities to congregate without the prying eyes of white people?"

I laughed. "Something like that. But it's not as segregated as it sounds. Whenever events happen like your summits, events that are usually catered to people who don't look like us, Black people will always find a way to feel welcomed and included. Even if we have to create it."

"I see," Will said, nodding.

"But it's not a 'Black folks only' thing. Everyone is welcome so long as you leave the drama at the door," I said, waving at the sight of Malika and Jeff.

Malika came rushing over. "You made it!"

"We did!" I said, leaning in to give Malika a hug. Will and Jeff did the manly handshake that seemed universal amongst most men.

"You guys clean up well!" Malika complimented.

"I have to say the same about you!" I said, gesturing at her outfit. She wore a gold, backless jumpsuit, showing off her body that rivaled Angela Bassett's.

Malika Conyers was the kind of woman who, no matter how fabulous and put together she was, never made another woman feel less than in her presence. I admired that about her. In fact, I admired everything about her. She was the kind of self-made businesswoman that little girls looked up to and aspired to be. I would kill for the opportunity to pick her brain for business advice.

This arrangement with Will was exposing me to people and opportunities I wouldn't have been able to access on my own—at least not this quickly. Will wasn't just providing the finances to take my business to the next level; he was also showing me a vision of the life I could one day have. It gave me hope for something I hadn't dared to dream of before now.

Music began blasting over the speakers, and the crowd went crazy as DJ D-Nice was announced. Malika and Jeff seemed to go into a trance as Beyonce's version of *Before I Let Go* began playing.

"Sorry, guys!" Malika yelled. "It's mommy and daddy's night out, and this is our song!"

Will and I laughed as they ran to the dance floor to join the crowd. "This is fun," Will said as he grabbed two glasses of champagne from a waitress passing by.

Apparently, this party was being thrown by another VC firm that was trying to make a name for themselves. When you were a newcomer in spaces like this, it was customary to throw parties and give free gifts to ensure your name was remembered when the event was long gone. And since DJ D-Nice was the hottest thing amongst people in these crowds, I had to give it to whoever organized the party. It was impressive.

The song changed to Usher's *Yeah!*, and Will's facial expression turned confused at the sight of the crowd parting into two lines. "What's going on? Did something happen?"

I looked at Will and then back at the crowd. "You're kidding, right? You're telling me you don't know what's happening?"

His eyebrows shot up. "Am I supposed to know what's happening?"

I laughed. "Oh my goodness, Willow Huntley! Have you never seen a Soul-Train Line?"

Will's face lit up with recognition. "Oh! Yes! I've seen these before."

My grin turned devious. "Good! That means you'll catch on really quickly."

Before he could protest, I took Will by the hand and dragged him to the dancefloor, making sure to stand right next to Malika and Jeff so they could see us.

"Timantha, what the hell are you doing?" Will asked, panic in his voice. "I don't dance!"

"It's easy! We got this! We're a team, right?" I said, jabbing him in his side to let him know we were up next.

When it was our turn, I grabbed Will by the hand and told him to follow me. "Step to the side, then step together. Step to the side, then step together!" I said, as we glided down the Soul-Train line to the rhythm of the boogity beat!

Even Jeff was impressed with Will, who didn't miss a beat while dancing. People kept coming up to us, commending Will on his impressive dance moves. I tried to get him to join me in the Electric Slide and Cupid Shuffle, but he said Soul-Train Lines were where he drew the line.

Will maintained a quiet confidence throughout the night. No one would have suspected he was full of nerves. We mingled and were introduced to various important people, but Will hadn't said much to anyone. He simply stayed close to me, possessively, quietly claiming me while simultaneously seeking comfort from my presence.

We didn't go to the dance floor for the rest of the night, but whenever a nice song played, we found ourselves swaying to the beat. With him standing behind me, his arms wrapped around my waist, he held me close and planted sporadic kisses up and down my neck. Watching him come alive and let loose as we grooved to the music was a refreshing change. It felt like he trusted me with his vulnerabilities, and I was determined not to let him down.

"Let me take you home," he pleaded, his arousal painfully pressing into my back.

I pulled my phone out and checked the time—it was just after ten o'clock. "How about thirty more minutes? I want to make sure we aren't leaving so much earlier than Malika."

He let out a heavy, sexually frustrated sigh. "Fine. Can I get you a drink? I need something cold to calm me down."

I turned around, reached up, and planted the biggest kiss on him.

"What was that for?"

"For you trusting me!" I said, smiling. "And I'll take a chardonnay!" I continued, before making a beeline to the restroom.

"Oh! Tim! Are you going to the ladies' room?" Malika asked, and I held out my arm for her to grab so we could walk linked. Will and Jeff made their way to the bar.

As we were walking to the back of the building, arm in arm, Malika leaned in to whisper-yell, "You know, everything I thought I knew or assumed about your husband is being shattered every time I see you two together. It just seems so real and organic. You two remind me of me and Jeff when we first got married."

"Oh really? How so?" I asked nervously, instantly feeling terrible about the lie we were perpetrating.

"Jeff was a stiff and stuffy man when we met. A nerd among nerds, okay?" she said, laughing. "But once he trusted me, he came out of his shell and became my best friend. Then he asked me to marry him."

Every time I saw Malika and Jeff together, I got the sense that they were real in a way few got to experience in a lifetime. Their natural connection and the way they vibed with each other was so aspirational. But I couldn't help but wonder what she saw between me and Will since everything about us was fake. At least that's how it started. Now the lines were blurred and the way this man couldn't get enough of me felt real. *Too real.*

I was fixing my makeup in the bathroom mirror when an unfamiliar voice sounded from behind me. "So this is what he chooses to pull off his little schemes?" the woman asked, but it came out more like an observation than a question.

I looked up behind me in the mirror, then turned to face the blonde woman who stood there. She was beautiful, very well dressed in a chic, black bandage dress, looking like she belonged in rooms like this.

"Excuse me? Do I know you?" I asked, because clearly she had the wrong person.

"He's always had a soft spot for charity cases," the woman continued, not bothering to answer my question.

I calmly placed my clutch under my arm and my hand on my hip. "Little girl, you have thirty seconds to tell me who you are and what the hell you're talking about or—"

The woman folded her arms across her chest. "Or what?" she challenged.

She took a step back and began body checking me as if she was sizing me up. "The notorious Will Huntley. Most eligible bachelor in his world, and *this* is what he chose. I heard rumors about him actually settling down, but I didn't believe it. But seeing him in that ridiculous outfit with you on the dance floor was all the proof I needed," the woman said before lowering her voice. "Too bad I'm one of the few people here who knows it's all a lie," she said, and the woman's words were finally starting to make sense. She was talking about my arrangement with Will.

I began panicking as she chronicled everything she knew about Will. "Everyone at his firm knows that Will pays whores to attend these events with him as his little playthings. You're the first one he's actually used to get ahead in business. I would say I was impressed, but it was silly of him to bring you to *my firm's party* tonight."

Just as she'd made that last statement, Malika stepped out of one of the bathroom stalls. Panic spread across my face. Had she heard everything this woman had said?

"Jessica Lucas! Great party tonight!"

The woman, who I now knew to be Jessica, turned from me to face Malika. "Malika Conyers! So glad you were able to make it! I see you brought a guest."

Malika looked between me and Jessica. "You two know each other?"

"Oh no! I just met this … Jessica Lucas, is it?" I asked, extending my hand to the woman for a handshake. She looked down at it as if it was contaminated.

She turned to Malika. "I noticed she was here with Will Huntley, and I couldn't help but introduce myself. I wanted to see who she was … what her angle was?" *No this bitch didn't.*

"Well!" I said nervously. "I've got to get back. I'm sure Will is looking for me."

I turned and nearly tripped over the garbage can on my way out the door when I heard Jessica say, "Mmmhmm."

When I walked out of the bathroom, Will was standing near the door, waiting for me with my drink in hand.

I downed the chardonnay, emptying the glass in one gulp before turning to Will in pure panic. "Somebody named Jessica Lucas just approached me in the restroom. Apparently, this is her firm's party, she knows we're not married, and I just left her standing there with Malika Conyers."

"Fuck!" Will cursed. "Tell me what she said, exactly."

Chapter Twenty-Four

Will

I usually loved being right, but this time, it made my blood boil. Letting my guard down had, predictably, invited trouble, and trouble had shown up at the worst possible moment. I couldn't believe I hadn't run into Jessica Lucas all week; that should have been my cue to stay vigilant. Just because she was out of sight didn't mean I was safe. I should have known better.

Attending this party should have been research for me as well. I should have investigated the host and identified the key players. If not for gathering intel, then at least to gain an inside track on the business contacts who would be there. Instead, I had been so focused on giving Timantha everything she asked for that I'd neglected the basic principles of doing business in environments like this. It was a cut-throat world, and there was no room for feelings or distractions.

We were driving back to our hotel and, even though the night air was cool, sweat was running down my forehead. "Who is this Jessica person?" Tim asked. "She seemed to take my being with you personally."

I let out a sigh. "She's someone I used to work with. She used to shamelessly flirt with me, and when I didn't give in to her advances, she didn't take the hint. So, after I came home one night to find her on my doorstep in a trench coat with nothing underneath, I reported her to HR. She didn't take that too well."

Timantha let out a sarcastic laugh. "You think?"

"What did she say to you, Tim?"

"Just that everyone knows you bring women to these events as 'playthings,' but I was the first that you'd ever involved in your business dealings. She couldn't wait to tell me she knew we weren't really married. And I'm pretty sure she called me a whore!"

I reached out to grab her hand, fully expecting her to recoil, but she didn't. "I'm sorry about that. You know that's not the truth, right?"

She cut her eyes at me. "Which part?"

"All of it. I mean, you know about the women, but you also know I don't bring dates for the reasons she's implying." I leaned in and kissed her gently. "And you're certainly not a whore. If she weren't a woman, I would've done a lot more about her calling you that."

"Thanks, Ike Turner, but I can handle myself," she said, smirking.

"What about Malika? Do you think she heard anything?"

"I honestly couldn't say. She seemed oblivious to our conversation when she and Jessica started talking, but I ran out of there so fast I can't be sure what happened afterward. I just knew I needed to get to you so we could strategize."

I grinned. "We? Are you coming around to being my accomplice finally, Timmy?"

She turned to look at me, and I swear each time she smiled felt like the first. "Mr. Willow Huntley, when you align yourself with a Black woman, what you will always have in abundance is support," she said, and my heart warmed at her words.

I'd intentionally avoided relationships. But being here with Timantha, feeling her unwavering support and partnership, even after everything she endured—being kidnapped and forced into this situation—I couldn't quite explain why. Maybe it wasn't relationships I was avoiding. Perhaps I was steering clear of relationships that didn't look and feel like this—safe.

"And you still insist on calling me Timmy, huh?" she joked.

"I can't help it. Just like everything else when it comes to you, I can't help myself."

She squeezed my hand gently. "But seriously, what are you going to do about Jessica and your deal with Malika?"

I let out a sigh, the weight of the situation pressing down on me. "I need to call my sister to strategize, but I don't have much of a choice. I have to meet with Malika tomorrow and hope she doesn't suspect anything."

"If there's anything I can do, you'll tell me?"

I took her chin in my hand. "You've done so much already. I don't know how to repay you."

She raised an eyebrow. "I think it starts with depositing the rest of that money into my account," she said with a grin.

I knew she was joking, but her words still stung. The fact that money was the first thing on her mind cut deeper than I cared to admit. I wanted her to see me for who I truly was, not just my wealth, and using money to attract her had been a mistake. A mistake I regretted deeply now that I was falling for her. It felt like she was falling for me too, but was it for the right reasons? I wanted her to want me for me, not for what I could provide. But what did I expect when I'd led with my wallet from the start?

When we got back to the hotel, Timantha did everything in her power to distract me from what was at stake.

"There is nothing you can do about anything tonight," she said, but that actually wasn't true. And it's why I needed space.

"Come to bed," she continued. "There's something I want to show you in chapter twenty-five of my book."

"It's tempting, but I need to call my sister. It's early morning where she is, and I've got to get into this with her ahead of the pitch tomorrow," I snapped, and I could practically hear her heart breaking from the rejection.

It was happening—I was becoming the man all the women I dated ended up hating. The one they left when it was all said and done. Whenever things got challenging and my focus was pulled in too many directions, something always suffered. And it was usually my intimate relationships. I couldn't understand why I kept taking them for granted, despite my crippling fear of losing them. It was like watching an inevitable train wreck; I saw the collision coming from a mile away, yet I couldn't stop neglecting the relationship long enough to prioritize the one I claimed to love. I didn't know how to turn off that part of me, but I knew I didn't want Timantha feeling that way. I didn't want her going to sleep feeling rejected by me.

"I get it," she said, her voice laced with defeat. "Tomorrow is a big deal, and you've got to be on your A-game. I'll see you in the morning?" She began walking toward her bedroom, but watching her walk away like that felt all wrong.

"Timantha," I called out. She stopped but didn't turn to face me. "Where do you think you're going?"

She turned, confusion etched on her beautiful face. I closed the distance between us in a few swift strides. Without hesitation, I claimed her mouth passionately, leaving no doubt about my desires or intentions.

"I'll be off my calls in about an hour. And when I'm done," I whispered against her lips, my voice husky with need, "I don't want to see you anywhere else but my bed. Is that understood?" She corrected her motion, and I watched as she walked into the bedroom. *My bedroom.*

The city lights of Paris flickered outside my hotel window, casting a restless glow across the room. Now that Timantha had disappeared into the bedroom, I was free to fully freak out and panic.

I paced back and forth, the phone clutched tightly in my hand. The ring sounded endless until, finally, Chloe's familiar voice came through the line.

"Will? It's late where you are. What's going on?"

"Chloe, I need you," I said, trying to keep the panic out of my voice. "Timantha ran into Jessica Lucas, and if we had any doubts before, we can now be certain that she's trying to sabotage my deal with Malika Conyers."

There was a brief pause on the other end, and I could tell that Chloe was choosing her words wisely. She let out a sigh. "What did she say?"

"She's threatening to reveal that my marriage to Timantha is fake. If Malika finds out, it's over. Everything I've worked for will be destroyed."

I wasn't just worried about this deal. My entire reputation would be ruined if anyone learned about this ludicrous charade I was playing in Paris. I'd be the laughing stock of my industry, and Chloe would be ruined simply by association. As a man, I'd recover and be relegated to some locker room banter. A woman attached to anything scandalous usually always meant absolute ruin. I couldn't let that happen to Chloe. Not after everything she'd done for me.

Chloe's tone softened. "Let's take this one step at a time before we completely freak out, shall we? How's Timantha handling all of this?" Always the mother figure, Chloe was worried about everyone but herself.

I couldn't help but smile, despite the tension twisting in my gut. "She's been incredible. More than I ever expected. Honestly, she's handling it exceptionally well."

Since Chloe was my best friend, I ran down the events of the week with her, including the hilarious debacle that went down with the baby. When I told her that Timantha had actually gotten me to dance, she was floored.

There was a knowing lilt in Chloe's voice. "Sounds like you two are getting along better than *just* partners in crime. You aren't falling for her, are you, Will?"

I hesitated, the admission almost too much to bear. "Maybe. I don't know. I mean, we've been spending so much time together, and it's ... different now. But what if she doesn't feel the same way?" I asked, sounding like a little schoolboy with a crush.

"Will, you've got to let your guard down," Chloe said, her words both soothing and firm. "Not every woman is going to be like—"

"I know, Chlo," I cut her off, not wanting to hear her say the name. I'd heard it enough for one week. For a lifetime.

Chloe's voice became even more commanding and firm but was still laced with the gentle care of a sister. "She's not *her,* and you're not Dad." I flinched at her words.

My father was the kind of man who could never commit to one woman, not even to my mother. His wanderlust and insatiable appetite for new experiences, both romantic and otherwise, led him away from us more times than I could count. I remember the hollow look in my mother's eyes whenever she would find out he was in Italy, or some other far-off place, with yet another woman. When my mother was dying of ovarian cancer, he was nowhere to be found. While she battled for her life, he was gallivanting in Europe, blissfully ignorant—or perhaps willfully so—of the pain and suffering he'd left behind. His absence during those final days was the ultimate betrayal, and even in death, my mother's heart was shattered by his indifference.

As Chloe's words tried to take root, I suddenly realized that my avoidance of commitment was also rooted in the scars left by my father's behavior. I didn't want to end up like him, a man who left a trail of broken hearts and unfulfilled promises. I had witnessed my mother's heartbreak too many times, the silent tears she thought I didn't see, the brave face she put on for our sake. The thought of someone I cared about being heartbroken by my actions—or worse, my absence—was unbearable. It dawned on me that this fear was yet another barrier between me and Timantha, a barrier I needed to break down if I ever hoped to find true happiness.

"Be honest with her," Chloe continued. She deserves to know how you feel, and you might be surprised at how she feels in return."

"What if it ruins everything?" My voice trembled. "What if she laughs in my face or thinks I can't be trusted after everything I've done?"

"Or what if she feels the same and has been waiting for you to make the first move and say how you feel?" Chloe's words echoed through the line, filling the empty spaces of my doubts.

I sighed, feeling the weight of the world pressing down on my shoulders. "You make it sound so easy."

"It's not," she admitted with a soft laugh, "but it's worth it. And you should also come clean with Malika. She needs to hear the truth from you, not Jessica."

I nodded, even though she couldn't see me. A spark of determination ignited in my chest. "You're right. About everything."

"I know! I'm usually always right." Chloe's smile was almost audible. "Tell her how you feel. And Malika with the truth. If she's the right partner for our business, her reaction may surprise you."

Taking a deep breath, I felt a wave of resolve wash over me. "Thanks, Chloe. I don't know what I'd do without you."

"You'd be a mess, that's for sure," she teased gently. But she was right, nevertheless. "Now go, fix this before Jessica ruins everything."

I ended the call, staring out at the city lights with renewed determination. The hardest battles were always fought with the heart, and I knew that this time I was ready to fight for what truly mattered. I had to face Timantha, confess my feelings, and then come clean with Malika. The stakes were high, but for the first time, I felt a glimmer of hope.

With one last look at the Paris skyline, I steeled myself for what lay ahead. The truth, no matter how terrifying, was the only path forward. And for Timantha, for my future, I was ready to take that step.

Chapter Twenty-Five

Timantha

This man embodied everything I'd ever dreamed of in a book boyfriend. His looks, his commanding presence, and that enigmatic dark side had me convinced he was straight out of a romance novel. The way he shattered my body with mind-blowing pleasure, only to tenderly piece me back together with gentle caresses and sweet whispers, was intensely erotic. And I was far from satisfied.

While we lay entangled in the sheets, our bodies still humming from the aftermath of four rounds of intense pleasure and six mind-blowing orgasms, I could sense a tension in Will that hadn't been there before. His touch was tender, his lips brushing against my skin in a way that both soothed and set my nerves alight, but there was something more, something unspoken lingering between us.

I felt him shift beside me, his arm tightening around my waist as if to anchor himself to this moment. His breath was warm against my neck, yet I could feel the hesitation in his every exhale. It was as though he was on the verge of saying something important, something that weighed heavily on his mind. Each time he opened his mouth, though, the words seemed to falter, caught somewhere between his heart and his lips.

"Will," I whispered, my voice barely more than a breath in the darkened room. "What is it? You can tell me."

He pulled back slightly, his eyes searching mine with an intensity that made my heart clench. For a fleeting second, I thought he might finally say what I had been longing to hear, the confession that mirrored my own hidden feelings. But then, just as quickly, he leaned in and pressed his lips to mine, a kiss that was more desperate than passionate, as if he was trying to drown his words in the act.

His hands roamed my body, gentle yet insistent, each touch a distraction from the truth I could see swirling in his eyes. Every time I tried to push, to coax out the words he so clearly wanted to say, he would silence me with a kiss, a caress, pulling me back into the physical, where our connection was undeniable and uncomplicated.

It was frustrating, this dance of avoidance, and I felt my own fears mirroring his. I wanted to tell him how I felt, to lay bare the emotions that had been growing with each passing day, but the fear of rejection, of ruining what we had, held me back. It was easier to lose ourselves in the physical than to face the vulnerability of our true feelings.

So we remained locked in this silent struggle, our bodies communicating what our hearts were too afraid to voice. And in those moments, as we clung to each other in the darkness, I wondered how much longer we could keep this up, how much longer we could deny the truth that simmered just beneath the surface.

I'd asked him to reveal more of his kink, to show me how it played out in the realm of desire, but he kept saying no, insisting it required a level of trust and commitment we hadn't yet achieved. I couldn't complain—everything we were experiencing was already driving me wild. But there was something irresistibly enticing about the forbidden nature of it all. The way he spoke about it made me ache to understand what it would take to reach that level of trust and safety with him. The man was a mystery that had me burning with curiosity, and I was eager to unlock every part of him.

With today being Will's big meeting with Malika Conyers and her team, I wanted to make the morning perfect. I woke up early to order breakfast for him, only to find that he was already gone. He'd left a note saying he couldn't sleep and had gone to the hotel gym to clear his head. After the incredible night we had and the work he put in, how on earth was that man not able to sleep?

I was doing some light packing, arranging the clothes Will had gotten me in preparation for our Sunday departure, when I heard a knock on the door. It was still early, eight in the morning, so I wasn't sure who it would be. When I opened the door, one of the men from Will's security detail was looking at someone's ID, but the guard's large frame blocked my view. Once he turned to me, I saw who it was.

"Jeff, what brings you by?" I asked, suddenly feeling underdressed in my yoga pants and matching sports bra set.

"I'm sorry to just stop by like this. I was hoping I could catch you alone?"

My eyebrows knitted together. "Uh, sure? Come in," I said, opening the door to invite him in. I flashed the security guard a knowing stare as if to say, *"You'd better be on guard."*

Everything about the night before was rushing through my mind. I couldn't calm my nerves, worried he was coming to confront me about the lies Will and I had told to get into Malika's good graces. My heart raced with anxiety, bracing for the fallout of our deceit. But nothing could have prepared me for what he was *actually* going to say.

We walked over to the sofa, and I gestured for him to have a seat. "Can I get you anything to drink? Coffee, perhaps?"

"No. I'm fine, thank you. This won't take long."

That was ominous. "Okay. What's this about, Jeff?"

Jeff let out a sigh, his look concerning and serious. "I consider it my job to protect my wife—not just her person or our household, but her business interests as well."

My heart began racing. *Shit. He knew.* "Jeff, I—"

He held up his hand, signaling for me to let him continue. "So, when I see two people who we've otherwise never met or even been in the same circles with cozy up to me and my wife out of the blue, I have questions."

I was paralyzed with uncertainty, my mind screaming for Will to burst through the door, rescue me, and tell me what to do. Should I confess everything? Let him keep talking? The tension was unbearable. I could feel disaster looming, and all I could do was brace myself for the inevitable impact.

I took a deep breath, and what came out next was both unimaginable and unintended at the same time. "Jeff, I know we lied about being married, but it's not what you think," I blurted out.

But Jeff said something at the same time.

I shook my head and furrowed my brow, "Wait, what?"

Jeff's face turned dark, his expression cold. "I asked you what you knew about Will's father. But what did you just say to me?"

I froze, confusion and panic battling for dominance. "Will's father?" I echoed, my voice barely above a whisper. "I-I don't understand. What does he have to do with anything?"

Jeff's eyes bore into mine, unyielding. "Embezzlement, Timantha. Will's father is in prison for embezzlement. Did you know that?"

The room spun, and I gripped the edge of the sofa to steady myself. Embezzlement? Prison? "No, I didn't," I managed to say, my voice trembling. "I had no idea."

Jeff leaned back, crossing his arms. "I find that hard to believe. You and Will insert yourselves into our lives, lie about being married, and now you claim ignorance about his father's criminal past?"

This is where the fairytale came to a crashing halt. Where the glittering facade of my Parisian adventure was shattered into jagged pieces. Of course this was all too good to be true. What was I thinking by not looking into everything there was to know about Will? How could I have been so naive, so blinded by the magic of our whirlwind romance that I didn't even consider that there were shadows lurking beneath the surface?

Now, the questions swirled around me, each one more unsettling than the last. What other secrets had Will been hiding? How deep did his father's misdeeds run, and how were they connected to the man I thought I was getting to know?

The revelation that Will's father was in prison wasn't the shocking part. I grew up in the inner city; many of my childhood

193

friends had been to prison. What truly troubled me was the fact that someone with a father in prison had the means and capacity to kidnap me and whisk me away to another country. It suggested that there could be even more danger lurking that I wasn't aware of or didn't see coming.

I felt a wave of nausea wash over me as I wondered what I had gotten myself into. Who had I really attached myself to? More importantly, what was Will's connection to his father now that the truth was out in the open? Was he still in contact, trying to cover up old tracks, or was he genuinely trying to distance himself from a tainted legacy? The questions gnawed at my mind, each one more unsettling than the last.

Each possibility was a thorn pricking at my heart and making me question everything I believed about us. "I swear, Jeff, I didn't know," I insisted, desperation creeping into my voice. "Will never mentioned it. I thought … I thought you were here because of our lie about being married," I stuttered.

Jeff's eyes narrowed. "It wasn't. But it only proves my point even further. I came over here because I needed to know if you're a threat to my family and my wife's business. Now it seems I have my answer."

I swallowed hard, feeling the weight of his words crush down on me. The truth. Jeff got up and walked toward the door, but turned and said, "Of everything I thought you were going to say, I didn't think it would be this—that your marriage was fake. Because what Malika and I observed between you two, that was the one thing that seemed real."

My heart sank as Jeff walked out the door.

Chapter Twenty-Six

Will

Despite the rounds of pleasure I'd taken Timantha through, I still couldn't sleep. She was laying peacefully on my chest, her soft, rhythmic breaths a serene lullaby against the chaos in my mind. I couldn't help but be tormented by the looming fallout from everything we had done. Everything I had done. None of this would have happened, my life and livelihood wouldn't be hanging in the balance if I hadn't been so desperate to win, so desperate to prove myself.

I traced the curve of her shoulder with my fingertips, a gentle caress that belied the tempest within me. If only I could turn back time and undo the desperation that had led me here. But there was no going back, and I was determined to shield Timantha from everything that might come next.

She was just starting a new business, one that I had vowed to help her with. If everything blew up in my face, she wouldn't want or need my name associated with hers. She would want to protect her reputation from this kind of scandal, and I should have considered that from the beginning. Her business and her goals didn't deserve to suffer because of my carelessness and selfishness. Despite all my efforts to prove I wasn't thoughtless and self-serving like my father, I was doing exactly the opposite.

Somewhere deep down, I secretly hoped that by the end of this week, Timantha might want to date me seriously. I'd even imagined planning a grand gesture straight out of a romance novel, where I'd get down on one knee and propose that she be my girlfriend. But if I ruined her—if her reputation suffered before she ever got a chance to make a name for herself—she wouldn't want me. And I had to accept that as a consequence of my own actions.

Timantha stirred slightly, her lips parting in a contented sigh. That's when I decided to go to the gym to try to settle my mind. I didn't want to wake her with my inability to sleep.

"Willow Huntley! Funny running into you here! What a coincidence!" Her voice pierced the quiet of the hotel gym, instantly triggering a headache.

"Jessica. Something tells me it isn't a coincidence at all," I replied, irritation seeping into my tone as I continued my pace on the treadmill.

"What can I say, you got me!" she confessed with a smirk. "I just wanted to see how your little pitch was going with Malika Conyers. I had the most interesting conversation with her last night."

I stopped the treadmill abruptly, the machine's hum fading into the tense silence. Panting from the workout, I stalked over to Jessica, each step deliberate with my gaze fixed on her. "What do you want, Jessica? What is your angle?"

Jessica Lucas had a menacing presence I couldn't shake. Her dark blue eyes, cold and calculating, always seemed to be plotting something sinister just beneath the surface. I couldn't forget the vindictive glint in her eye the day I got her fired; it clearly still fueled her vengeful obsessions.

She lingered in my life like a shadow, her threats veiled in seemingly casual conversations, her smiles always too sharp, too knowing. The way she twisted a simple comment into a dagger aimed at my most vulnerable spots kept me constantly on guard. I knew she was capable of wreaking havoc on my carefully constructed world, and that knowledge gnawed at me, especially now when I had so much to lose.

Her smile widened, a predator sensing weakness. "Oh, nothing much. Just curious if she found out about your *marital status.* It would be such a shame if your deal went south because of a tiny detail like that."

My fists clenched at my sides, the urge to lash out barely contained. "Being so new in this business, trying to make a name for yourself by sabotaging others to potential clients is just as damaging as the harm you're trying to inflict," I said, peering down into her blue eyes. "It makes you look just as untrustworthy."

She laughed, a cold, mocking sound. "Oh, Willow, always so dramatic. Can't take a little competition, I see."

I leaned in closer, my voice dropping to a dangerous whisper. "Listen carefully, Jessica. If you ruin this for me, I will make sure your career is over before it even begins. I don't care what lengths I have to go to or who I have to take down. Stay out of my way."

I wasn't above enlisting the help of my connections to dig up dirt, and Jessica knew that all too well. She'd witnessed firsthand the lengths I would go to when crossed, which only made her bold and brazen demeanor more concerning. She had to know that ruining even one deal for me would unleash a hellfire on her world like she'd never seen. The fact that she was still willing to provoke me, to dance so close to the edge, meant she either had something up her sleeve or was more desperate than I thought. Either way, she was playing a dangerous game, and I was prepared to make sure she lost it.

Her eyes narrowed, but she didn't back down. She shifted on her heels and rested her right hand on her hip. "The thing is, Will, there's a difference between trying to sabotage someone and simply making sure my *friends* are fully aware of who they're getting into bed with."

I raised an eyebrow. "Still upset that I wouldn't get into bed with you, huh?"

"Don't flatter yourself. Getting the opportunity to stretch my wings in this new venture was the best thing that could have happened to me."

I nearly laughed. "Are you trying to convince yourself or me?"

She smirked. "And then there's the little thing about your father."

"What about him?" I snapped back. I had done a lot of work and had spent thousands of dollars hiring cyber experts to distance myself from my father's misdeeds. The only thing worse than Malika Conyers finding out about my lie about being married was finding out about my father being in prison.

Nobody wanted to work with the child of a criminal, especially one whose father had committed such heinous acts. Corporate espionage, embezzlement, and even rumors of hiring a hitman to eliminate his business partner once his crimes were uncovered—my father had done it all. Chloe and I spent years painstakingly rebuilding our reputations, distancing ourselves from the taint of his name. We had even gone as far as changing our last name, desperate to sever any association with him and the dark legacy he'd left behind. It was a struggle to regain trust in a world that judged us by his sins, but we fought tirelessly to carve out a new identity, one that wouldn't be overshadowed by his monstrous deeds.

I was preparing to hand out even more threats when I heard my phone beep, signaling a text message. I held my hand up in Jessica's face while I fished my phone out of my pocket.

Tim: *Get back here. NOW!*

I didn't even bother to respond. I brushed past Jessica, grabbed my workout bag, and left her standing there. Her message was cryptic, not clueing me in on anything that was going on. But it didn't matter. In a short amount of time, Timantha had reached a place with me where I knew I would drop anything and everything for her—no questions asked.

Chapter Twenty-Seven

Will

When I got back to our hotel suite, my security detail handed me an envelope. I didn't look at it or open it to see its contents. I simply stormed into the room to get to Timantha.

"Tim. What's wrong?" I asked, my voice edged with concern as I took in her tear-streaked face.

She was sitting on the edge of the bed, her laptop open next to her, displaying a plethora of news articles and background checks. Her eyes were red, tears still threatening to spill over.

"You didn't think it was important to tell me everything?" she said, her voice shaking with emotion. "It's not that you lied about who your father was, Will. It's that you didn't think I deserved the whole truth from the beginning."

My heart sank as I took a step closer to her. "Timantha, I didn't want you to judge me by my father's actions. I've spent my entire adult life trying to prove that I'm different. That I'm better."

She looked at me and let out a sardonic breath. "And you think hiding the truth makes you better?"

"No," I admitted. "I realize now that everything I've been doing has proven the exact opposite. I was so desperate to escape his shadow that I became a reflection of it. And I'm sorry,

Timantha. I should have told you everything from the start. I should have trusted you with the truth."

Tears welled up in her eyes again, and she looked away, her hands trembling. "I've been doing my own research, Will. I wanted to know everything about the man I'm falling for. And finding out this way ... it hurt."

I was preparing to apologize once more when my conversation with Jessica Lucas flashed in my mind. "Timantha, what made you look into my father anyway?" I asked, realizing it was beside the point, but the timing was all too coincidental.

She looked up at me. "You didn't know?"

I furrowed my brows. "Know what?"

"Jeffrey Conyers was here. He knew everything about your father."

My heart pounded so violently against my ribcage that I feared it might bruise. Jessica wasn't going to be petty enough to simply reveal my fake marriage to Malika; no, she was far more cunning than that. She was taking a more insidious route, one that would raise their suspicions in a completely different way. Exposing my father's identity and his heinous crimes would surely destroy any trust they had in me. The revelation of who my father was would taint everything, making them question my integrity and intentions.

Suddenly, I heard a gasp come from Timantha and my attention snapped to her. Terror was etched across her face. "Oh no. Will. There's more ... shit!" she cursed.

"Timantha, you're scaring me."

She began pacing back and forth. "Shit! Shit! Shit! Shit! Shiiiiit!" she yelled erratically, and I walked over to steady her.

I placed my hands on her shoulders and positioned her to face me. "Timantha. Breathe." She inhaled and then let the breath out. "Tell me what happened?"

Her next words were an almost unintelligible stream of consciousness. But I heard what was important. "Okay. So. I thought Jeffrey Conyers showed up to confront me about our fake marriage. He wanted to speak to me alone, and I thought it was like a brotha-to-sista-girl thing so I let him in, and when I thought he was about to rip into me about lying to him, I maybe sort of blurted out that we weren't really married."

Fuck. Me. Now I was the one pacing in panic. "How was that the *first* thing you blurted out? Of all things, *that* was what you said?"

"I'm sorry!" she whined. "How was I supposed to know that your father was a criminal with known ties to the mafia? Because you certainly didn't tell me!"

I lowered my head. "I know. And I promise you I only concealed it out of shame. Nothing else."

She folded her arms across her chest. "Whatever, man."

I grinned, and where I was initially blinded by panic and rage, awareness suddenly hit me. "You wore that when he was in here? Alone?" I asked, scanning her body in the form fitting yoga pants and sports bra she was wearing.

She shifted. "Yes. I didn't realize he was coming or obviously I would have changed."

"You should have made him wait," I growled.

She put her hand on her hip, and I sunk my teeth into my bottom lip. "Excuse me? I think you need to put the caveman on hold since you've clearly forgotten that you have a deal that is about to blow up in your face!"

She was right. She'd just told me that Jeff and likely Malika knew our secret, and there I was turning into a possessive neanderthal. Women. Always throwing me off my game.

"What's in the envelope?" Timantha asked, reminding me that my security detail had handed it to me when I'd gotten to the room.

Reluctantly, I tore it open, my heart pounding as I read the contents. "It's an invitation," I said, my voice thick with unease. "Malika and Jeffrey Conyers want to meet for brunch." My eyes flashed to Timantha and then back to the piece of paper. "They want both of us there."

Timantha looked at me, her brow furrowing. "What does that mean?"

"It means that this isn't going to be the business meeting I anticipated," I said, a tremor in my voice. "What could they possibly want with both of us?"

She walked toward me and placed both hands on my chest, a move that was tender as much as it was seductive. "The only thing left to do now is face it."

My eyes met hers. "Together?" I didn't care how desperate it came across. I needed her to know that I needed her with me.

"Together," she agreed, and I dipped my head to pull her into a kiss.

My hands began to instinctively roam her hips, and she melted into my embrace. A moan escaped her lips, and I hardened at the sound. She broke contact and then peered into me. "Fucking lie to me again and I'll knee you in the nuts."

Chapter Twenty-Eight

Will

My heart was racing as Timantha and I walked into the hotel restaurant, the same place where we'd first run into Malika and Jeff. My mind was spinning with anxiety now that Malika and Jeff knew our secret. I glanced at Timantha, who offered me a reassuring smile, but it did little to calm the storm inside me.

We spotted Malika and Jeff at a corner table, their expressions unreadable. As we approached, my steps grew heavier, each one echoing the weight of my dread. We exchanged polite greetings before sitting down, the silence around the table thick and oppressive. No one spoke, each of us waiting for someone else to break the tension.

Under the table, Timantha gently stroked my hand, her touch grounding me in the moment. She squeezed my hand reassuringly before looking up and breaking the silence.

"Malika, Jeff, I think it's time we clear the air," she began, her voice calm but firm. "I want to take full responsibility for the lie about us being married. It was my idea. I thought it would help Will make a strong impression."

I cleared my throat. "Timantha—" I interrupted, trying to stop her, but she squeezed my hand and continued with her confession.

Malika's eyes narrowed slightly, but she remained silent, listening intently.

"Will has had nothing but amazing things to say about the company and the culture you've built, Malika," Timantha continued, "and I wanted to do everything in my power to help him succeed. I thought that by presenting ourselves as a stable, committed couple, it would reflect well on him."

Other than my sister Chloe, no one had ever come through and showed up for me like this. For so long, I believed that people only looked out for themselves, and I'd insulated myself from the world with that belief. But sitting here with Timantha, watching her take on the responsibility of the lie to protect me, was something I never thought I'd experience. Her selflessness was a revelation, a beacon cutting through the fog of my cynicism.

"When you align yourself with a Black woman, what you will always have in abundance is support." Her words from last night surged to the forefront of my mind. They resonated deeply now, a stark reminder of the strength and loyalty she embodied. Timantha was proving that she was more than just a partner in this charade; she was my ally, my confidante, and perhaps something even more profound.

Timantha's voice softened, filled with genuine admiration. "I've been a fan of your products for years. My entire family uses them. I admire what you've built, and I wanted Will to be part of it. He deserves this chance."

Malika's expression softened a fraction at Timantha's words, but the hurt was still evident. "I appreciate your honesty, Timantha. And it's flattering to hear that you're a fan. But this lie ... it's hard to get past."

Finally, I spoke up, realizing it was immature to allow her to shoulder this all on her own. "Malika, if I may, I know the

206

lie was absolutely ridiculous and asinine to think we could get past you. You are far too intelligent and important for us to have believed that this was the way to impress you," I said, pointing to Timantha's ring on her finger.

"I'm glad you recognize that," Jeff chimed in. "The lie wasn't as insulting as the fact that you thought you could get one over on us."

"I understand that, Jeff. And while Timantha is taking the responsibility, as a man, I can't let that happen. I should have come to you, man-to-man, once I realized this was all getting out of hand." Jeff nodded, and I had a good mind to warn him against cornering my woman alone in a hotel room again, but I figured it probably wasn't the time.

"And to think we thought the information about your father was the most scandalous thing we'd heard about you," Malika said, and it almost felt like she was joking.

"Malika, I can assure you that—"

She held up her hand to silence me. "Don't even mention it. When Jeff told me what Jessica Lucas had done, cornering him to give him that information, I knew something was off." She took another drink of her juice. "Besides, I don't trust people who feel the need to sabotage others to get ahead."

"What about people who lie about being married?" I joked, hoping it wasn't too soon.

"And about that!" Malika said as if she'd been reminded of something. "How is it that you two seem so perfect together but your relationship is fake? Jeff and I were discussing it, and you couldn't convince us that what you have isn't real."

207

Timantha's grip on my hand tightened, and she looked Malika straight in the eye. "This connection between us is definitely real, and it's grown stronger because of what we've been through this week. But the lie was never meant to deceive you in a malicious way. It was a misguided attempt to present ourselves in the best light."

My heart warmed at Timantha's words. She felt the same way about me, and I couldn't be happier. In that moment, the deal could be all but done and my company in ruin, but this woman sitting beside me felt something special for me too.

Jeff, who had been mostly silent, finally spoke. "That doesn't negate a very important fact, though. Honesty is crucial in any partnership, personal or professional. We need to know that we can trust you, Will."

"And right now, we just aren't sure we're able to," Malika added. "But it has nothing to do with your father, we need you to know that. We don't believe people should be punished for the sins of their parents. Otherwise, Jeff and I wouldn't be here today."

I took a deep breath, feeling the weight of their scrutiny. "I understand. I've spent my entire adult life trying to prove that I'm not like my father. I didn't want my past to define me, to overshadow the hard work I've put in to build a different future. But I realize now that hiding the truth was a mistake."

Malika sighed, her gaze softening. "Will, it's clear that you're sincere in wanting to prove yourself. And Timantha, your support and honesty speak volumes about your character. This isn't an easy situation, but I appreciate you both coming clean."

As we finished brunch, the tension began to ease, replaced by a tentative hope. Malika was firm in that she needed time before taking on any investors. Seeing the lengths that I was willing to go to get her business made her pause even harder. She took time to evaluate everyone thoroughly and, even though it didn't reflect the best things on me, I was glad she was being more scrutinizing.

We got back onto the elevator, headed back up to our room to debrief, and my heart was overflowing with gratitude while it anxiously beat through the fabric of my shirt. But Timantha was a vision of poise of confidence. "You didn't have to do that, you know?"

Timantha had put herself on the line for me without a second thought for her own well-being. I was grateful, but part of me hated that she felt the need to do so. Women were always sacrificing themselves for the people they loved, and the world often repaid their sacrifices with brutality. Despite knowing this, Timantha still came through for me, standing firm and unyielding in her support. Her courage and selflessness were both humbling and infuriating, making me more determined than ever to prove that her faith in me wasn't misplaced. *But first ...*

I looked at her while she scrolled her phone, oblivious to the heat of my gaze. "Do what?" she asked, shrugging.

I grabbed her phone out of her hand and placed it in my suit pocket. "Wha? Hey!" she yelled, lunging toward me to grab the phone, but it was already deep inside my pocket.

"Look at me when I address you, Timmy."

Her lips parted, but words never formed. The elevator dinged, and we both looked up to see that we were passing the

209

third floor. Heat filled the elevator car as memories of the first night we shared in that same space came crashing down on me. She felt it too.

"You didn't have to stand up for me back there. I was fully prepared to take responsibility for it all. I can take that kind of hit to my reputation, Tim. You can't."

She stepped back, putting distance between us until her back was against the wall of the elevator. "You're welcome, by the way," she said sarcastically.

I took a step in her direction, then two more until I stood over her, my left hand braced against the wall above her head as I peered down at her. I reached around her waist and pulled her hips toward me so she could feel my *gratitude*. Fifth floor. "You keep surprising me," I murmured, my voice low and rough. "Easing your way into the crevices of my heart that I desperately need to keep closed off."

Her breath hitched, and she looked up at me with those eyes that saw right through my defenses. The tension between us was electric, charged with unspoken emotions and desires. I could feel her warmth against me, and for a moment, the weight of the world seemed to lift, leaving just the two of us in this intimate space. And I was done pulling away or fighting myself every time I got close to letting her in.

I was ready. She was wearing a white pencil skirt with a matching crop top, and I cursed trying to figure out how to touch her without getting her dirty. *Fuck it,* I thought as I bent down to claim her mouth. I used my right hand to grip her thigh and bring her leg around my waist.

"Shit, you're sexy," Timantha whispered, and I growled at the compliment. Eighth floor.

She held her leg in place around my waist as I unzipped my pants to relieve the aching in my groin. "Condom," I cursed. "Fuck, it's in the hotel room." I felt like a teenager on prom night as I stood there with my dick literally in my hand.

"Birth control," she panted, and it was all the consent I needed to charge into her.

I lifted both of her legs so high around my waist that I heard the slit in her skirt rip. She anchored herself around me, her arms wrapped tightly around my neck, her legs gripping my waist with a fervent strength. She was so small compared to me, delicate and light, yet filled with a fire that matched my own. I could hold her by her waist and glide her up and down my length with ease. And so I did, savoring her inch by inch as she moved up and down.

I steadied her against the wall so I could reach behind to lock the elevator in place. If someone stopped this car and attempted to get in, I'd murder them. We were stopped on the eleventh floor, but I was nowhere near close to being done with her. I returned all of my attention and effort to Timantha, and the look in her gaze was enough to push me to my release.

In and out, I rocked into her as if I was trying to give her all of me. She felt so good that I knew I wouldn't be able to keep this slow and sensual pace for long. My desire for her was a roaring inferno, consuming me from the inside out. I wanted her completely, utterly, in a way that would ruin her for all other men. This moment was only the beginning, a prelude to the hours that would follow, where I'd claim her again and again, leaving her breathless and yearning for more.

211

I couldn't take it anymore. I buried my head in her neck, licking and sucking as I shattered every wall—hers and mine—that had been built around us. "Shit! Will! I can't be quiet. Someone might hear!" she pleaded, but I took it as an enthusiastic plea for more.

"Good," I bit back. "Let everyone know whose you are."

"Fuuck! Yours. So fucking yours!" she yelped, and it caused me to go harder. Faster. Until we both erupted in untamed ecstasy.

For the second time that week, I'd done exactly what the tabloids expected of me. I'd taken a woman in a public place and didn't care one bit who saw or knew.

Chapter Twenty-Nine

Timantha

After what felt like an hour, Will and I went back to our suite and picked up right where we'd left off. It was like a damn of passion broken inside him, because even though we'd slept together before, this time felt like more. Like surrender. I woke up wrapped in Will's arms, the remnants of our passion lingering in the air. The sunlight filtered through the curtains, casting a warm glow over our intertwined bodies. We had spent the day making love, exploring each other's bodies, but also sharing our stories, peeling back the layers that made us who we were. We hadn't come up for food, water, or air in hours.

Will's hand trailed lazily along my back as we talked about our childhoods. He spoke of his sister Chloe, the only constant in his turbulent life, and the shadow of his father's crimes that had always loomed over him. I shared memories of my own family, the simple joys and struggles that had shaped me into the person I was today.

Unable to take the growling of our stomachs, we ordered room service. I'd stepped out of the shower, draped in the hotel robe, when I caught a glimpse of Will watching me. "What?" I asked, grinning.

His voice was always sharp and commanding but, as the night deepened, Will's voice grew softer, more vulnerable. "I've never wanted to consider a serious relationship before," he admitted, his eyes searching mine. "Until I first laid eyes on you.

And now that I've tasted you, I don't want anyone else to know what it's like to touch you."

His words sent a shiver through me, both thrilling and terrifying. We had all but confessed our feelings for each other, and yet, a part of me wondered if our dreams were too unrealistic, too fragile to withstand the harsh light of reality.

I sat next to him on the bed, lathering my body with my favorite scented body oil. "You almost sound like you mean that."

"Do I strike you as the kind of man who says things he doesn't mean?"

He had a point. "All of this," I said, gesturing at the opulence of the suite. "This trip, this suite, your plane, even how Malika Conyers and her husband handled our lying to them … it all feels too good to be true. Like a fantasy." The kind of fantasies I only read about.

"Is there a question in there somewhere?" he asked with a grin, then he pulled me on top of him, causing my robe to open.

Will's eyes darkened at the sight of my breasts peeking out from the robe's opening. In a swift move, he dipped his head to lick a trail up the center of chest, and I threw my head back, allowing for the robe to spill open.

He began untying the belt of the robe, freeing what was left hidden behind its fabric, and I moaned at the sensation of him drawing a nipple into his mouth. "Does this feel real? True, sweet girl?" And *fuck* if I wasn't going to come from the sound of those words on his tongue alone.

Room service arrived at the door, and when I tried to stop, Will pinned me to him, my legs wrapped around his waist. "They'll see! Hear us, Will!"

"How many times do I need to tell you that I don't care who hears or sees what's mine? I don't care who hears you scream my name," he said through gritted teeth as he bit down on my nipple, and I gasped from the ecstasy of it all.

"Shit! Will!"

"As long as mine is the only name on your tongue, the whole world can hear."

I felt him reach for the hardness that was threatening to tear a hole through his sweats while I simultaneously heard the room service cart being wheeled in.

We were in Will's room on his side of the suite when I heard, "Room service!" from the other side of the very open bedroom door.

Will brought his lips close to my ear. "Do you understand me?" he whispered.

"Ye—shiit!" I whimpered, as he stole the very breath from my lungs as he slammed himself into me.

The movement from the other side of the wall stilled as I'm sure the outburst startled the butler. But just as soon as they'd stopped, they resumed their work. I could hear them organizing the plates and forks at the dinner table the way Will had requested. The picture of professionalism, I had to hand it to them. They seemed as if they didn't hear a thing.

As Will positioned himself on the edge of the bed, me straddled on top of him, he used his hands to guide my hips up and down his length. "That's it, sweet girl. Squeeze every ounce of pleasure out of me." And so I did.

I tightened my legs around his waist, using the force to give me more control over my movements. I did as he said, squeezing him over and over as I rode him up and down. I buried my head into his neck and bit down on his shoulder, chasing the motion with my tongue. And Will unraveled inside me, giving me more than I expected, given the amount of times he'd already satisfied me.

When we'd decided we'd had enough and my legs could no longer perform the job for which they were hired, Will carried me into the living room area where the butler had set up a delightful spread for our dinner. Pancakes.

The next morning, I wandered around our hotel suite, packing my things. As I carefully folded designer outfits and placed them next to the stunning dresses and luxurious accessories, a wave of uncertainty washed over me. How could I ever return to my normal life after being exposed to all of this opulence? The life I had before seemed a distant memory, overshadowed by the intoxicating luxury I had been plunged into.

I glanced at Will, still sleeping peacefully, his face relaxed in the early Sunday morning light. We came from such different worlds. Could we truly bridge the gap between us? Would the reality of our lives shatter the dreams we had built together in this gilded cage?

I sighed, folding the last of my clothes. Despite the doubts gnawing at the edges of my mind, I knew one thing for certain: I didn't want to let go of what we had found. The connection between us was too strong, too precious to abandon without a fight.

The deal with Malika Conyers might have fallen through, but her genuine interest in what came next for me and Will was unmistakable. She even handed me her personal contact information, suggesting we keep in touch. This unexpected gesture made me wonder about the possibilities. What would it mean for Will if we ended up together for real? How would our relationship impact his world, and could we truly build something lasting amidst the chaos? The thought was both exhilarating and terrifying, leaving me to ponder our future as I clutched Malika's card in my hand.

Will stirred, his eyes fluttering open as he looked at me with a sleepy smile. "Morning," he murmured, his voice husky from sleep.

"Morning," I replied, forcing a smile to hide my turmoil.

He sat up, rubbing his eyes. "What's on your mind?"

I hesitated, then decided to be honest. "You keep saying that you want us to try something real, but I'm just wondering how we're going to make this work. Our lives are so different, Will. What if reality tears us apart?"

He got out of bed and walked over to me, pulling me into his arms. "I will scorch the earth before I allow anything in it to tear us apart. Is that understood?"

I didn't know words so menacing could sound so sexy. "Understood," I said with a grin.

"Good. Now let's get dressed and finish packing. We need to be at the air strip soon, and there are a few things I'm dying to try out on my plane."

Chapter Thirty

Will

Six Months Later

"So what airline can I book a flight on your plane through, Will?" Timantha's mother asked, and I nearly choked on the piece of cornbread I had in my mouth.

"Well, Ms. Spellman—"

"Now, what did I tell you about calling me Ms. Spellman like I'm a school principal or something? Call me Mama!" the saucy, southern woman chided.

"Sorry ... uh ... Mama ..."

Timantha finally walked in and rescued me. "Leave the man alone, Mama. I promised him he wouldn't be bothered too much."

Timantha handed me a glass of sweet tea, and I'd never get used to the way she served me. It always made me feel uncomfortable, but she said she enjoyed it. The only thing my mother ever served my father was a stiff drink from time to time. I didn't think I'd enjoy this domesticated lifestyle, but having Timantha around had made life simpler and easier in a way I never imagined.

Standing in the backyard of Timantha's family home, the warm, savory scents of barbecue filled the air. Laughter and the sounds of children playing floated around me, blending into a

219

symphony of joy. According to Tim, I should feel honored to be here today for this celebration, because not just anyone was invited to Black family cookouts. Taking in the scenery, I could understand why.

There were so many things happening that felt celebratory and sacred at the same time. Crowds of people danced all around with no designated dance floor in sight. A grumpy, old man guarded the grill, never letting anyone touch it but always throwing a piece of meat on anyone's plate who walked by. And grown men were in the corner of the yard nearly in tears over a game of spades. I looked down to see that Timantha's hand was nestled comfortably in mine, and I couldn't help but smile as I looked at her.

After we got back from Paris, Timantha kept her word and didn't report me for kidnapping her. She hadn't even taken all the money I offered. Not wanting our relationship to mirror the ending of *Pretty Woman*, she chose to donate it to Biddy Mason, a local charter school that thrived on community support. From that moment on, everything between us felt instant and organic.

We threw ourselves into each other, our lives intertwining in ways I hadn't imagined possible. We began dating seriously, and she dove headfirst into working with a developer to design her app. She still ran her matchmaking business, and whenever she met someone I knew to be a notorious playboy, I made sure a security guard went with her to keep an eye on things. I'd become even more jealous since she and I started dating.

The deal with Malika Conyers might have fallen through initially, but it wasn't the end of the road. My company faced some turmoil, but we managed to recover. I designed a strategy for Malika to acquire a smaller company that would help her expand into the European markets. She jumped at the opportunity, and since then, we'd built a solid working relationship. Timantha had even babysat for Malika a few more times, a testament to the trust and bond we'd all developed. *Pretty sure J.R. hasn't been airborne since Paris, though.*

Timantha was everything I needed in my life, and I didn't even know it. She brought balance to my chaos, light to my darkness. Watching her interact with her family, seeing her laugh and smile, filled me with a warmth I hadn't known I was missing. I realized then that I wanted to make this feeling permanent. I wanted to show her just how deeply in love with her I was.

"Hey, what's that look for?" Timantha asked, noticing my lingering gaze.

"Just thinking about how lucky I am," I replied, pulling her closer.

I was preparing to pour my heart out to her when screams erupted from all around us. Startled, I looked around to see what all the commotion was for. "What's going on? Is everything okay?"

Timantha smiled and shook her head. "This again, huh? Do you not recognize the song that just came on the radio?"

I paused to take in the melody to see if I could guess what it was. A grin slowly began to spread across my face. "This isn't the same version as before," I said.

"I know! It's the best version." She beamed before grabbing my hand and dragging me to the area of the backyard where everyone had congregated.

"Do you remember the moves?" she asked, taking my hand in hers as the crowd parted, forming two separate lines.

"Oh, I remember the moves, Timmy. Do you?"

"Okay then! Show me what you got, Willow Huntley!" she belted as we began making our way down the Soul-Train line to Franky Beverly and Maze's *Before I Let Go.*

Timantha and I stayed at her mother's house until everyone had left. She washed dishes, and I helped her cousins put away all the chairs and tables. On the drive home, she'd fallen asleep in my lap and I marveled at how easily we'd settled into this ... *relationship.* Being with her was the easiest thing I'd ever done. Her maturity, her sense of humor, her fierce attitude, and the way she handled business made my mouth water. I was determined to keep her in my life for as long as I could. For as long as we both shall live.

Timantha stirred, awareness flashing across her face as she realized she was no longer in the back of my SUV. Her eyes widened in panic, darting around until they landed on me, a grin plastered across my face.

"Will? What's going on? Are you kidnapping me again?" she asked, half-joking, half-serious.

I chuckled, nodding. "Yes, but this time, I've cleared it with your mother and your staff to make sure you have everything you need."

Since Timantha was building a business and an app, she could no longer afford to be whisked away without notice. So this time, I made sure to be a little more considerate with my plans as I took her away for the week.

Her eyes softened with relief and curiosity. "Where are we going this time?"

"Italy," I replied, my grin widening as I watched her eyes light up with excitement.

She jumped into my arms, her joy infectious. "Italy! I can't believe it!" She kissed me, her lips warm and eager. The kisses quickly became heavy and lustful, her body pressing against mine with a fervent need that mirrored my own.

Unable to resist, I scooped her up, her legs wrapping around my waist as I carried her to the back of the plane, to the master bedroom.

I still hadn't fully introduced Timantha to my darker realms of *play,* but after six months and now crossing the line of meeting her family, I figured it was time to unleash more of myself to her.

"I've got a surprise for you, sweet girl," I said in her ear. My flight crew disappeared as they saw Timantha's breast spill from out of her tank top and into my mouth.

"Surprise?" she panted. "You mean a trip to Italy isn't it?"

I bit down on her nipple as her head flew back with pleasure. "Not quite all of it," I confessed.

I steadied her with my left arm around her waist while my right hand traced a path up her thigh and straight into her wetness, and fuck was she ready for me.

"Have we reached that level of trust yet?" Timantha whimpered, hinting at her need for taking things deeper and darker in the bedroom.

She'd been asking for a while and growing more and more frustrated that I didn't invite her into my dungeon. Little did she realize that my refusal was part of the play as well.

My eyes darkened with passion. "I think we have, sweet girl," I replied, effortlessly plunging my fingers in and out of her. "First, I'm going to make love to you," I whispered against her skin. "I'll worship every inch of your body and make you beg for more."

She pulled the bottom of my earlobe into her mouth. "Fuck yes, Will," she whispered.

"I'll lick and suck your clit, kissing you in ways that will make you cry out in pleasure, filling you with sensations you've never experienced before."

I stopped and opened the door to the master bedroom. "And then … when I've made you feel like the most beautiful and treasured jewel in the world, leaving you breathless and utterly undone, I'll ruin you, my sweet girl."

I looked into her eyes, searching for any hesitation. "Do you trust me? Will you trust me to do that, Timmy?"

She whispered back, her voice filled with anticipation, "Yes."

As we tumbled onto the bed, our laughter and passion intermingling, I knew that with Timantha, life would always be an adventure, filled with unexpected detours and exhilarating moments. And I wouldn't have it any other way.

The End

About the Author

Taccara Martin is a contemporary romance writer and an award-winning fiction podcast producer who has, along with her husband, Kenyon, gained over 100,000 social media followers using the timeless magic of words.

A survivor of domestic and narcissistic abuse, Taccara infuses her narratives with a deep passion for healthy love, weaving stories that mirror the intricate realities of relationships, even when they aren't perfect.

She's married to her "forever book boyfriend" and openly shares how Kenyon fuels her endless romance inspiration. Together, they live just outside Atlanta, Georgia and share a blended family of six amazingly creative kids.

Visit TaccaraMartin.com for more information.

Made in the USA
Columbia, SC
27 November 2024

47775491R00126